HIT AND RUN...

Maybe Camille didn't hear the car because she was still chattering to herself.

Maybe she didn't see it because she was looking the other way.

Either way it didn't matter. For all Camille knew was that out of nowhere, almost as if it had dropped down from Mars, a car was suddenly speeding towards her.

Camille froze. She couldn't put it all together. Time went into slow motion. She saw blinding light, round and hot as the California sun. She saw broad metal bumper and an endless expanse of windshield. She saw someone behind a steering wheel, and stared right into the driver's eyes.

Then everything went into super speed.

There was a scream of brakes, and a sound that Camille realized was her own scream. And then she felt a terrible, breath-sucking smack in her side before she sensed that she was being hurled into outer space.

Look for Samantha Crane

...ON THE RUN
...CROSSING THE LINE
...ON THE EDGE
...ON HER OWN*

by Linda A. Cooney
bestselling author of the FRESHMAN DORM *series*

*coming soon from HarperPaperbacks

SAMANTHA - CRANE - ON THE EDGE

Linda A. Cooney

HarperPaperbacks
A Division of HarperCollins*Publishers*

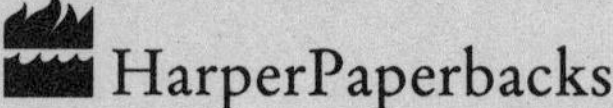
A Division of HarperCollins*Publishers*
10 East 53rd Street, New York, N.Y. 10022-5299

ISBN 0-06-106411-4

Cover illustration by Trevor Brown

First printing: October 1996

Printed in the United States of America

Visit HarperPaperbacks on the World Wide Web at
http://www.harpercollins.com/paperbacks

❖10 9 8 7 6 5 4 3 2 1

1

"Walk in with me, Sam."

"Jen, it's just a school dance."

"I can't do this alone."

"Jen."

"Everybody's talking about me!"

"Jen, people have other things to talk about."

Sixteen-year-old Samantha Crane stared at her beautiful best friend, Jennifer Dubrosky. It was dance night—party night at West L.A. High. But poor Jennifer was acting like she was being forced into a torture chamber. Sam believed in taking care of her friends. She was known for being sympathetic and loyal. But she wasn't sure Jen was even listening to her.

"Where's Camille?" Jen fretted. Jen glanced around, searching for the third person that made up their tight girlfriend triangle—super-achiever, Camille Weeks.

"I'm right here, Jen." Camille joined them,

suddenly appearing around the corner of the school gym. She gave a warm, reassuring smile. "Sam's right. It's just a dance. Let's go in and find Kenny. If we're not having a good time, we can just turn around and leave."

Thank you, Camille, Samantha Crane wanted to chant. Instead she and Camille peeled Jen away from the concrete wall outside the West L.A. High gym. Ten feet away, couples lined up, waiting to enter the gym's double doors. Music thumped. Two seniors wiggled to the Friday night party beat.

Jen stood frozen, as if she were about to be sent to juvenile hall.

"Nobody even knows what happened to you," Samantha promised.

"They know," Jen swore.

"How could they know?" asked Camille.

Jen shrugged, then blinked up at the dark sky. "They just know."

Sam exchanged glances with Camille. Jen had wedged herself between a trash can stuffed with crepe paper and a fallen spirit sign that said, *West L.A. Cobras Slither to Victory*.

Still, it was hard *not* to believe that people weren't talking about Jen. They were gossiping about how Jen had been duped into almost posing for a pornographic film. They were saying *slut, fool, airhead* behind Jen's back.

And Jen knew it. She looked windswept and combustible. Her silky, blond hair was plastered across her cheek. Her crushed velvet dress was blown tight. Her blue eyes darted. Even the ribbons around her neck fluttered, so that nothing about her seemed calm.

Camille Weeks, on the other hand, was her usual bundle of focused energy. School talk-show host, top student, fast talker, walker and thinker, she wore a tailored gold blazer over electric blue leggings. Her cornrows were unbeaded, pushed back by a wide purple headband. Her compact body was poised for action, while her dark eyes focused only on Jen.

Sam felt like she was halfway between scattered Jen and on-track Camille. Sam's single long earring—a painted bangle that Jen had made in art class—swayed. Sam's stomach churned with worry about Jen, while her bicycle shorts, heavy socks and lace-up boots were planted firmly on the earth. Sam wanted to be a solid rock of loyalty for Jen, but she also had her own wacky life to cope with.

"Jen, I'll stick with you," Sam promised. "And really, people are just talking about the track meet this afternoon. They're talking about how Dylan won that race, and about who made finalists for the Governor's Award."

Camille, who was one of those finalists for that prestigious award, grinned and waved. *"Moi?"* she said.

Sam ignored her. "Jen, people just want to know about who said hello to whom, who likes which guy and who is dressed like a dork."

Jen glanced down.

"Girlfriend, you look great," Camille assured her.

Sam nodded. Jen was one of the most beautiful girls in the entire junior class. "Come on."

"Okay."

Sam and Camille each took Jen's hand. Heading for the gym, they had to fight a gust of wind that swirled up leaves and candy wrappers. By the time they reached the brightly lit double doors, the dance line had disappeared. Even the ticket table was unmanned. The three friends stood alone, digging into their pockets for the dollar admission.

Suddenly junior Dawn Warrington swung around from inside the foyer, popping open a soda can. As Dawn flopped down into the ticket-taker chair, she guzzled Pepsi, then wiped fizz off her upper lip. She snickered when she saw Jen.

"Look who's here!" Dawn giggled, referring to Jen with mock surprise. Dawn had the personality of a brushfire—dangerous hot barbs alternated with smoky looks. She was a follower of snobby Kristine Moore, who was practically on a campaign to make life miserable for Sam and her friends.

Dawn wore a spirit choker necklace in the shape of a cobra. All this West L.A. High *rah rah* was starting to get on Sam's nerves, especially when Dawn's greeting was about as spirited as the hiss of a rattlesnake.

"It's Jennifer!" Dawn spit.

"Perceptive, Dawn," Jen managed to shoot back. "You're a certified genius."

Dawn's eyes blazed behind tinted contact lenses. Kristine had a devoted group of followers, and Dawn was groupie number one. Dawn was obviously kowtowing to conform to Kristine's recent spirit drive. Sam wondered if Dawn would tint her eyeballs in spirit colors just to please powerful Kristine.

"Jen, I just didn't know you were back in school," Dawn said.

"I'm back," Jen managed. She slapped down her dance money then took a deep breath. "What exactly are you trying to say, Dawn?"

"Oh, nothing, Jen." Dawn sighed. "I just know you stayed home for a week after . . . *it happened*. I didn't know if you were really in school again."

Camille leaned over Dawn. She was only five-foot-one, but had a seven-foot personality. "Unless you're even dumber than I think you are," Camille quipped, "Jennifer is standing right in front of you."

Dawn's mouth flapped open.

"She is even dumber than we thought she was," Sam snarled. She grabbed the tickets out of Dawn's hand. "Look, she can't think of anything else to say."

Without any further comment, Sam and Camille pushed Jen into the gym foyer. They folded down on a single bench, sandwiching Jen between them and ducking under the crepe paper snakes that hung from the ceiling. Sam and Camille practically removed Jen's shoes for her, then stowed all three pairs of footwear—Sam's combat boots, Jen's ballet slippers, and Camille's purple loafers—in a communal cubby.

"Uh oh," Camille pretended to worry. "We're all asking for it. Dawn will tattle on us to Kristine. *Tsk, tsk.*"

Jen smiled—the first smile Sam had seen from her that whole week. "Just let her try."

"Dawn is out of control," Sam muttered. "And if Kristine tries anything, we'll give her the same treatment. You were great, Camille."

Camille let out one of her big round laughs, which echoed even over the blaring thump, thump of the dance band.

Bolstered by Camille's good cheer, Sam led the way into the gym. The gym scene made her smile, too. Technically, it was a spirit dance, which meant it had been organized by Social Activities Coordinator Kristine. But Sam could instantly see that Kristine hadn't managed to control everything, or dampen what Sam considered the *true* spirit of West L.A. High.

Kristine had certainly overseen the decorations—the usual blue-and-gold streamers fluttered from the backboards. There were snake murals and snake charmer baskets in both basketball hoops. But West L.A. High's eccentric twists and odd details had made their marks, too—despite Kristine and her spirit monsters. Sam recognized a few youth center regulars bopping around to the music, as well as members of Club, Club, her school service club that was known for its eccentric members and important missions. In fact, Club, Club had provided the music, so the featured band was a makeshift quartet—King Cobra and the Destructos.

"Yes!" Sam grinned as she looked around.

A huge banner announced the dance theme in drippy blood letters. *Day of Destruction*—because *Destroy Downey* had been the chant at that afternoon's track meet. In addition, the entire West L.A. High campus was undergoing a destructive/constructive renovation campaign—the theater had just been revamped after an electrical fire. The girls' shower room was temporarily a pile of rubble, since it was in the process of being redone. A mural painted by the art club showed scenes of campus demolition, plus the usual L.A. landslides and floods.

But The Destructos' music didn't make Sam feel beaten down. In fact, the sound of it filled her with energy. And the sight of the musicians made her feel buzzy and light, too. Or rather, the sight of the lead guitar player, who was none other than Sam's friend/downstairs neighbor/soulmate/maybe more than that . . . Kenny Sando Wilson.

When Kenny spotted Sam, he lifted his guitar, bent a long, soulful E string, then pretended to play the guitar with his teeth. His face was lit by a strobe, but the blinking light couldn't disguise his part French, part Vietnamese, part African-American heritage. He wore an old-fashioned tuxedo jacket over his slim, bare chest, plus red tennies and shredded jeans. A top hat balanced on his light brown afro. The band was another of Kenny's thrown together garage bands—major guts and heart, over-the-top volume, but not too much attention to technical detail.

"KENNY!"

Samantha waved, then tried to shoulder her way across the dance floor to greet him. Camille broke away to hug friends from Brain Bowl, but Jen stuck with Sam, hanging onto the arm of the sweater Sam had tied around her waist. Sam felt like she was baby-sitting.

"Stick with me, Sam," Jen panicked.

"I will."

Between Jen and the couples flailing to the beat, Sam was moving pretty slowly. She hadn't even made it to the middle of the dance floor when someone else grabbed onto her. He hooked his arm into hers and twirled her around until she felt like she was stuck in a revolving door. Suddenly Jen let go and Sam spun in her stockinged feet. As she twirled, she realized that her life lately was one big Tilt-O-Whirl. Spin one way and look after edgy Jen. Twirl another way and greet dynamic Camille. Slide out to one side, and get thrown into the arms of unique, unpredictable Kenny. Slip in another direction and meet the alter ego of her love life—the junior who had just eased his arm around her—track star, Dylan Kussman.

"Hi." Dylan grinned, starting to dance with her.

Sam's head swam and she couldn't keep track of anyone. Dylan's freckled skin still looked flushed, although his hair was now neatly combed and he'd changed into corduroy slacks, a tee shirt and sweater vest. His feet were bare and he had a crepe paper Cobra draped over one shoulder.

"I didn't see you come in. Did you just get here?"

Sam nodded. Kenny kept watching her as Dylan took her hands and threw back his head. He began dancing with the same graceful energy that had fueled him to victory in the track meet that afternoon.

"Congrats on your race today," Sam yelled over the music.

Dylan grinned. Sam looked back and forth. Dylan and Kenny. Kenny and Dylan. Jen and Camille. Camille and Jen. That revolving door was spinning faster and faster. Sam wondered when it would suddenly stop and smack her in the face.

Sure enough, when Kenny spotted Dylan, he turned his back to the audience. Sam glanced back and forth between the two boys. Now her brain felt like it had gone into orbit. Kenny raised the volume on his amp.

TWAAAAAAAAANG!!!

"Anyway, yeah, I just got here with Jen and Camille," Sam yelled. And she'd since lost track of Jen.

"Jen," Sam mouthed.

No one was on her sweater tails now, she realized. But then she spotted Jen, just as Jen was waylaid by Rafe Danielson. Also a junior, Rafe had surfer blond hair that was perfectly straight, cut all one length so that it fell over one cheekbone. He always seemed to have a golden tan and an easy smile. He'd run well in the six-hundred-meters that afternoon, although he hadn't run as well as Dylan. Jen seemed pleased that Rafe was paying attention to her.

But Sam couldn't concentrate on Jen anymore. Dylan was the one who had triumphed in the six-hundred-meters that afternoon. Sam had been in the bleachers when he'd crossed the finish line, his red hair flapping, long limbs straining, his face tense with effort and concentration. Sam stared at him, taking in his green eyes and straightforward smile.

Just then The Destructos' song petered out, ending with an ungraceful drumroll. The keyboard launched into the next number. Despite Kenny's attempts to change the song order, a slow number began, with the keyboard player crooning a sultry vocal. Dylan didn't bother asking Sam to dance. He just looked at her and she was no longer caught in the revolving door. Taking a deep, shivering breath, she slipped her arms around his shoulders. His arms tightened around her back and she felt woozy as her face snuggled into the warm crook of his neck.

To Sam's surprise, she spotted Jen over Dylan's shoulder. Jen was slow dancing with Rafe. Rafe cocked his head so that golden hair covered half of his face. He pulled Jen in closer while Kristine Moore, Dawn and a few other Kristine groupies stared and gossiped from the edge of the floor.

Sam waved to Jen. She tried to take it all in. She saw a group of kids collecting near the door, passing something that looked like a liquor bottle. She tried to keep track of Jen and Rafe,

Kristine and Dawn. She could still see Kenny, although she'd totally lost track of Camille.

"I've missed you, Sam," Dylan whispered, as he pulled her closer.

Everything was spinning again and Sam couldn't do anything to make it stop. So she just closed her eyes and let the world whirl. But this was a different kind of movement. This wasn't being sandwiched between plates of cold glass and metal in a revolving door. This wasn't worrying about a freaked-out friend. Instead she took in Dylan's clean skin, silky hair and the slightly scratchy wool of his sweater vest.

Sam sighed softly.

This feeling was so frothy and light that she could spin right off the earth and into the smoggy L.A. sky.

2

Someone else was having a feeling too . . . but not a wonderful, spinning feeling.

No, this was a bad feeling.

Like the feeling you got when you were a kid, and they didn't pay attention to you. When they said you weren't good enough. When they said you had to do better.

And better was never good enough.

But there were ways to forget those feelings. Quick, quick. Make yourself forget. Make yourself look away.

Forget . . . forget . . .

Don't feel, don't feel.

Make it all go away.

And then a strong smell of alcohol. It brought tears to your eyes. Or was it from drinking or maybe something else. No way to know . . . already you were forgetting. That was fine . . . forget, forget, forget . . .

And then stumble out of the school. Go to the parking lot. Find your car. Get away.

But most of all . . . forget.

Outside the school, Camille Weeks *never* forgot anything.

She was in command and in control. Other kids were flaky about homework, deadlines, and curfews. Not Camille. People joked that they could set their watches to Camille's entrances and exits. They could set their *lives* to them. Camille never fell head over heels. She was too sensible for those kinds of feelings, too full of purpose and determined to leave her mark.

That meant exercising self-discipline. It meant paying attention to rules and to people. It meant ignoring some feelings and cultivating others. Camille didn't let romance turn her head, but if it came to getting extra credit in a class, then she could become downright *impassioned* over a homework assignment.

At the same time, Camille wasn't an icicle. She certainly understood what it felt like to be on the outside, so Jen's plight was hard for her. Camille wanted to be able to deny the whispers, but it wasn't possible. The whispers were there.

She wanted to be able to say, *Heck, these people are fools, just ignore them, girl.* Right. Bad things *had* happened to Jen. There was no good solution to what Jen was facing or how she was hurting. Time would solve the problem eventually, but it seemed fatally prim to say, *Oh, it's alright. Time heals everything.* That was a line right out of the *Parents All-Time Great Clichés* manual, and Camille was definitely not Jen's mom.

So maybe that was why Camille was leaving the dance early, even though she loved to dance. It was just too hard thinking and worrying about Jen. "Jen's okay," Camille chattered to herself as walked across the dark school parking lot, heading for her mother's Volvo. If she said it enough maybe it would be true.

Her loafers *clack-clacked* along the blacktop. Other than the wind and muted echo of Kenny's band, the parking lot was quiet and very still.

There were a couple of encouraging signs. Jen had been highly concentrated on Rafe. "Of course all we'll hear about now is Rafe this . . . Rafe that . . ." Camille shook her cornrows and laughed.

In fact by the time Camille had left the dance, Jen and Rafe had been acting like the couple of the semester. Sam and Dylan had been looking pretty cozy, too. Rafe and Dylan. Dylan and Rafe. Camille couldn't get either of them out of her head. But her boy preoccupation was totally different from Jen's or Sam's. Camille liked boys, but she also knew that boys could mess big-time with her goals. She tried to look at boys like a math equation.

"It's numbers," Camille said out loud.

The wind blew dust in her face as she stood in the middle of the parking lot, looking up and down the rows of cars.

"For me, it's all about numbers." Camille laughed again. She knew that was totally silly. It was as if she were playing a game. Everything could be controlled. If she understood the math of human emotion, then she could make herself a life that was perfect.

Yeah, right . . .

Camille was looking for the license numbers on her parents' Volvo. She'd driven solo that day to arrive early and drop off her confirmation as finalist for the Governor's Award.

"The Governor's Award. I want it, I want it," Camille chanted as she wandered down the rows of cars. "I want it more than any boy." She stopped at a dusty Jeep and traced 6 . . . 5 . . . 4 . . . 3 . . . 2 . . . 1 on its dirty back window.

"Blast off," she said, giggling. Then she reminded herself again, "It's all going to come down to numbers."

Camille was good with numbers. In fact she was good with all kinds of figures and facts. But it was numbers that were at the heart of the Governor's Award. First, the award meant money numbers. The Governor's Award would be given to one junior at each public California High School. No scholarship was directly attached, but everyone knew that winning the award would be a free ticket to his or her university of choice. Camille's family wasn't poor, but if she wanted Stanford or Yale, she was going to need some extra bucks.

Then there was the number six, Camille pondered, as she stared at the Jeep window.

There were six finalists. She was one. Dylan Kussman and Rafe Danielson had made the finals, too. Then there was social queen Kristine Moore, plus two other squeaky-clean, high-powered juniors—Suria Lu and Barry Barsumian.

This was where the real math came into play. Camille scribbled some more figures on the Jeep window.

One fifth of the score was grade average . . .

"Three point nine two," Camille mouthed as she calculated her own average on the glass. Her grades were the highest among the finalists, except for Barry the Brain, who had a perfect 4.0. But then you added in the twenty percent based on community service. Forget boring Barry in that department. In fact, none of the other finalists could compete with Camille there. Camille had tutored reading for elementary school kids, worked with Sam to help the local youth center, serve free meals to street people and raised money for AIDS.

Extracurricular activities were next—that category included athletic performance. Camille wrote for the school paper, had interviewed a teen TV star for a school talk show, competed in debate and Brain Bowl. On the other hand, Dylan and Rafe had just scored major points for track, and Suria was an all-city swimmer. Kristine had the lead in the upcoming school play, was Miss School Spirit and self-appointed Tsarina of social activities.

That left teacher recommendations—that fifth was totally unpredictable. And the last twenty percent was also hard to predict. The final fifth would be based on an upcoming speech on a topic relevant to American values. Camille loved public speaking and showing off her knowledge. She loved competition, showing off and taking up any kind of challenge. So there was nothing to be nervous about.

Phew.

Camille erased her figures on the Jeep window as she suddenly remembered that she hadn't parked in the lot at all, but had left the Volvo on a nearby street. She giggled to herself as she walked toward Bonita Place, where the back of the school bordered a quiet residential avenue.

"I'm nervous anyway," she admitted to herself. "It's like competing for Miss America." She laughed out loud at her own joke. "And I would definitely like to see Barry Barsumian in an evening gown."

Camille continued talking to herself. It was a habit she'd indulged in as a kid, and her mind and mouth were so active, that she usually kept up a constant chatter when she was alone.

"So, I've gone over all our strengths," she rambled as she stepped into the dark street. The lamp was broken and Camille had a hard time seeing the edge of the curb. "Now for our weaknesses. Okay. Dylan and Rafe are depending on their track scores, so they'll have to run really well." She giggled and tried to remember where she'd left her mother's car. "Suria definitely has the lowest grades. Barry only has grades. And Kristine Moore will have to prove that despite her beauty, brains, popularity and school service, she also has something resembling a heart."

Then Camille stopped, right in the middle of the dark street. "And me. What are my weak points?" she pondered. "Now that's the question for me to really think about."

For a brief, glorious moment, Camille felt like she had no weak points. She enjoyed a surge of confidence where she felt like anything was possible. Responding to a blast of giddy energy, she took off, running as fast as she could in the direction of her parked car.

Maybe Camille didn't hear the car because she was still chattering to herself.

Maybe she didn't see it because she was looking the other way.

Either way it didn't matter. For all Camille knew was that out of nowhere, almost as if it had dropped down from Mars, a car was suddenly speeding towards her.

Camille froze. She couldn't put it all together. Time went into slow motion. She saw blinding light, round and hot as the California sun. She saw broad metal bumper and an endless expanse of windshield. She saw someone behind a steering wheel, and stared right into the driver's eyes.

Then everything went into super speed.

There was a scream of brakes, and a sound that Camille realized was her own scream. And then she felt a terrible, breath-sucking smack in her side before she sensed that she was being hurled into outer space.

"AHHHHHHHHHH!"

Time stopped again.

Something hit the side of Camille's head. It came out of nowhere, attacked her and bit into her skull. The pain went into her head and down one side of her body. In that moment Camille realized that she'd hit the ground with her head, and her whole body was now stretched out in the middle of the dark street. Then she heard the car speed off.

Camille felt like she was on fire. Her stomach turned over as everything went black.

3

Rookie L.A. Police Officer Alison Crane had been thinking about her daughter.

"Samantha," she mumbled.

Alison and her partner, Officer Carlos Silva, were cruising La Brea Boulevard in their black-and-white squad car. Carlos, tall and beefy in his LAPD blues, stared out at the barely lit taco stands and gated-up clothing stores. When they passed the West L.A. Youth Center, Carlos cleared his throat.

"Did you say something, Alison?"

"Did I?" she wondered. "Oh, never mind. I'm just talking to myself."

"If you come to any amazing conclusions, let me know."

Carlos started whistling.

Alison's thoughts wandered. She was still new to the force. The only street officer who specialized in crimes involving juveniles, she was passionate about her job—even when she wasn't exactly sure what her job entailed. She'd saved teens from sexual exploitation and murder, but had also just given rides when kids got stranded. Alison would remind high school kids to wear bike helmets. She'd take runaways out for burritos. And maybe that was problem. While she was microwaving at the Seven-Eleven, her own daughter was home alone. If Sam needed someone to talk to, Alison would probably be on shift.

"Nothing much going on tonight," Carlos mumbled. He squinted into the dark, wrinkling up his round, handsome face.

Alison leaned her head on the window and nodded. "Maybe the wind blew all the crazies to Beverly Hills."

Carlos chuckled.

At least Alison could joke with Carlos now. In fact, she could finally walk through her precinct house and get, "How's it goin', Officer Crane?" instead of a leering, "Hey, honey." With Alison's last case, she'd scored a few brownie points—or maybe she should call them Boy Scout points, since her precinct was so overwhelmingly macho. Whatever her points were called, she'd busted a teen pornography ring. Sam's friend, Jennifer Dubrosky, had been drugged and almost been used as a model. Poor Jen had thought she was pursuing a legitimate Hollywood acting opportunity. Jen still seemed humiliated and hurt, but at least Alison and Sam had intervened in time.

As a result of solving Jen's case, Alison's

sergeant had invited Alison to propose new ideas for dealing with juvenile crime. Alison was actually being given some independence and some respect! Now she had to decide exactly what to propose, and what angle to pursue. Prevention? Juvenile counseling? Education?

"Hey Alison," Carlos said. "I hate to interrupt such a peaceful night with bad news, but . . . "

Alison focused her attention on him. His dark eyes narrowed as he gripped the steering wheel. "What, Carlos?"

"Remember Willa Van Landingham?"

"Of course." Alison would never forget Willa. Alison's first case had involved the murder of a teenager. Willa, a runaway from Oregon, had almost become a victim, too. Eventually Willa had left the streets of L.A. Alison had recently gotten a postcard explaining that Willa had gone back home.

Carlos turned into the Third Street McDonalds and headed for the drive-in window. He drummed the dashboard as they waited behind a stalled minivan. "I got some news about Willa, during a call about another offender."

"Willa wasn't an *offender*," Alison snapped. "She was a runaway."

"She's an offender now," Carlos tossed back. He jerked the car forward, then ordered coffee and hot apple pie. "Willa got picked up for shoplifting from the Mervyn's in Grant's Pass. She ended up in juvenile court."

Alison shot forward and smacked the radio.

She hated seeing troubled teenagers get thrown into the criminal justice system. Detention centers and juvenile homes just served to send borderline kids completely over the cliff. But if kids weren't detained or punished, they'd decide the justice system was a joke and feel free to experiment with more serious crime. "Did they take Willa away from home?"

Carlos paid for his food, then flinched when he burned his mouth on the pie. "Her family life stank."

"Carlos, she'd just been put with *foster* parents! She was back in school!" Alison grabbed his coffee and gulped it. "Why does this happen? She's not some dangerous psychopath. How could they let her get ground up in the justice system. She's just a messed-up kid!"

Carlos licked his fingers and pulled back into traffic. "Willa had a history of running away, and a prior for trespassing. Don't yell at me, Alison."

"Well, who else can I yell at?" Alison ranted. "Willa needs a home, friends and a sense of purpose. Now she really won't have a chance!" That thought made Alison wonder if her new idea shouldn't be some kind of nationwide program for runaways. Sure, there were safe houses and computer banks, but the LAPD had never come up with a good system of helping kids who ended up on the street. They just followed laws and procedures, even though those rules didn't always make sense when they applied to teens.

That was what was filling Alison's head,

when the call came over the radio. The voice of Leanne, the dispatcher, crackled over the speaker and in that instant, Alison's thoughts flip-flopped back to Samantha.

"There's been a hit-and-run accident on Bonita Place, just behind West Los Angeles High School. Alison, Samantha made this call. Your daughter wants you to take this ASAP. The victim is one of her friends."

"Ay caray," Carlos muttered in Spanish.

Even before Alison had signed off, Carlos had the siren blaring. He'd dropped his coffee cup and was speeding onto Melrose. For once the traffic was light. Alison held her breath as Carlos wove around trucks and sped through stop signs. In exactly six minutes, they came to a screeching stop on Bonita Avenue, behind the back of the school library.

Alison was out of the car before Carlos had come to a complete stop. A circle of students filled the streets, as well as a couple of teachers who held flashlights to warn oncoming cars.

"The paramedics are on their way," Alison announced as she rushed into the center of the crowd.

"Camille!" Alison gasped as she saw Camille's petite body lying on the asphalt. For some reason Alison had thought that the victim might be Jen. After everything else that Jen had been through lately, it seemed like Jen had become a walking disaster area. But Jen was nowhere in sight.

Instead it was super-achiever, always-on-top-of-things Camille. The only thing Camille was on top of now was Kenny's folded tuxedo jacket, which rested under her head. Camille was curled over on her side, with Sam's sweater draped over her middle. Camille's eyes were closed, and tears stained her dark cheeks. Dylan knelt at Camille's feet, while Sam and a bare-chested, shivering Kenny hovered at either side of Camille's bloody head.

Alison slid in next to Sam and flashed a light in Camille's eyes. Luckily, Camille flinched. She turned her head, exposing a bloody, grit-filled scrape that stretched from her temple to the middle of her cheek.

"Mom, I didn't move her," Sam promised. "She smacked her head. That scrape on her face is where she must have hit the hardest."

"We just got here," piped up a teacher in a West L.A. High sweat suit.

Alison ignored the teacher and focused her attention on the teens. Camille tried to sit up. "Don't get up, honey," Alison warned. "Wait for the paramedics."

Camille sat up anyway. She wiped her face, then seem stunned to find that her hand was covered with blood. She began to shake. "I'm okay."

"You're not okay," Carlos barked. "Stay down."

Camille seemed to get woozy and allowed Carlos to help lower her to the ground again. He knelt, too, and pulled out a small notebook. He began to jot down notes. "Did you see the car that hit you?" he asked Camille.

"No," Camille whispered. She seemed to fight a wave of nausea.

"I already asked her that," Sam said. She knelt next to Carlos and hovered over his shoulder. "Camille doesn't remember the car or the driver. She's not sure she even saw them at all."

Carlos gave Alison a look.

Sam went on. "The street lamp is broken, and the school light back here is burned out. If a driver came around that corner too fast, it would be easy to miss a pedestrian until it was too late." Sam looked at Kenny. "What I can't believe is that whoever hit Camille just drove off without stopping."

Alison took Camille's hand, which was cold and trembly. Camille had her eyes closed now, as if she were taking a nap. "How did you find her?"

A young-looking Asian girl spoke up. "Jay and I left the dance early. We were getting into my car, and I heard this scream. I came running and found Camille lying in the street. She was totally unconscious for two or three minutes."

Samantha interrupted. "Jay ran back to the gym. I overheard him telling Mr. Roder."

The teacher nodded.

"Jay and Lin heard the car drive away, too," Sam added. "They didn't see the car that hit Camille, but they heard it speed off. It left really fast. Right?"

Lin nodded.

Carlos cleared his throat. In the short time that Alison had been on the force, Sam had developed an uncanny sense for police work, too.

Alison was proud of Sam's insights and perseverance, but she also worried that Sam got too involved in her cases.

But that was yet another thing that Alison and Sam hadn't had time to talk about. And now certainly wasn't the time to catch up, especially since the ambulance had just turned onto Bonita Place. A moment later, two paramedics had unloaded a stretcher and were tending to Camille.

"I'll ride in the ambulance with Camille and call her parents," Alison assured Sam. "You and Carlos meet us at West L.A. General. Everybody else, please clear out of the street. Go on with your evening. Thanks for your help."

Alison broke up the crowd as Camille was loaded into the ambulance. She watched Sam glance back at Kenny, then at Dylan. A moment later Sam slid into the police car with Carlos and they were all on their way.

"What a day, Trash Man."

"What a night."

"What a weird, creepy, scary, horrible night."

Three hours later, Sam sat on the front stoop of her apartment building, a chunky Spanish two-story on Spaulding Avenue. She nuzzled Trash Man, the alley cat that she and Kenny had both adopted. Kenny sat next to her, his shoulder leaning against hers. He'd put on a heavy old fisherman's sweater and occasionally leaned over to scratch behind Trash Man's ears.

The wind tilted palm trees and tumbled branches along the street.

"How long will Camille be in the hospital?" Kenny asked.

"Just overnight if all the tests come back okay." Sam took a deep breath and stared at the parked cars. A sheet of newspaper skipped from windshield to windshield. "The hardest place she hit was her head."

"Not exactly the place you want to get hit hard."

"Of course, Camille has a . . . "

"Pretty hard head," they both said at the same time.

Then they just sat while the wind shook the petals off the rosebushes and made the birds-of-paradise wave. Kenny skated his fingers along the top of Sam's hand, then slowly wrapped his palm around hers. Sam gazed into the street again. For once, the traffic on Spaulding Avenue was light. Just one car sputtering and stalling, cruising for a parking space.

Sam had gone up to her apartment after returning from the hospital. But her mom had gone back to the station, and Sam hadn't wanted to stay in their second-floor apartment by herself. The wind made the windows creak. It swept the lawn chairs across the roof.

So Sam had used her special communication system to call down to Kenny—she whistled into the drain pipe that ran from her kitchen to Kenny's bedroom on the first floor. The wind had made her whistle sound like a coyote howl. Even wild Trash Man seemed spooked and, for once, was content to settle quietly in Sam's lap.

"Did you call Jen?" Sam asked Kenny. "She doesn't know what happened to Camille, does she?"

Kenny's brown eyes were glued to Sam. He looked sleepy and sad. "I didn't call her. And she probably doesn't know about Camille yet. She'd already left the dance when we found out about Camille. She'd left with Rafe."

Sam sighed. "Rafe is another worry. Jen's pretty vulnerable right now."

Kenny shrugged. "I think he's a good guy, although I don't know him very well."

"I'll call Jen in the morning." Sam fingered the earring that Jen had made for her. How could one person be so thoughtful, talented and gorgeous, and yet so insecure, mysterious and sad. Jen, Jen, Jen . . . "Maybe Rafe is just what Jen needs. Wouldn't that be weird?"

"Life is weird." Kenny sighed. "It's weird to think that Camille was just walking across the street, everything was hunky-dory, and the next second she's practically killed."

"It's even weirder to think that a driver could hit someone and just drive off."

"People can do strange things." Kenny nodded. "In a split second, your whole world can change."

Sam stopped breathing for a moment. Kenny was really locked onto her now. He kept staring, even when she tried to look away. Sam wasn't sure how to react. For so long, she and Kenny had been just friends. Then Dylan had come into the picture, and her relationship with Kenny had transformed, too. Sam liked the closeness and the sudden electricity between her and Kenny. Even so, she wasn't always sure that she really wanted to go from an easy, uncomplicated friendship into something more. She and Dylan, on the other hand, had started as something more, and Sam wondered if they would ever enjoy the ease of just being friends.

Kenny tipped his head until it rested on her shoulder. Then, to Sam's surprise, she was the one who went over the line. She just felt so warm with Kenny, so safe. She put her cheek against his, then initiated a short, light kiss. It was like melting into the wind, as if the rest of the world had been blown away and there was nothing left but her and Kenny.

Kenny pulled back and looked at her with hazy eyes. He touched her hair, then smiled. He was just leaning in to kiss her again, when Sam realized that someone was strolling up the walkway toward the apartment stoop. In fact, two people were approaching, fighting the wind and glaring at Sam.

"Well, well," sang Kristine Moore.

Sam was stunned to recognize Kristine's nasty, nasal tone. How Kristine could ever be playing the lead in the school play was beyond Sam. On the other hand, Sam knew exactly how Kristine had won the role, and it had nothing to do with her vocal talents.

"Sorry to break up this love fest," whined

Kristine, "but there was someone who wanted to drop by and see you."

Sam was still having trouble just focusing on Kristine. The rich social queen didn't exactly hang out in Sam's neighborhood. In fact, Kristine had never been to Sam's apartment. What was she doing there now? But then Sam took in the second visitor and her heart sunk. Dylan was standing next to Kristine. His hands were in his pockets. He looked like he wanted to crawl into his letterman's jacket and let the wind sweep him off.

Kenny inched away from Sam.

Kristine smirked. "Whether he *still* wants to see you, Sam, is probably a whole other question."

Sam no longer felt like she was spinning or melting. This was more like being dropped into a pit full of poisonous snakes.

"Dylan asked me to drop you off here on my way home," Kristine gloated. "We stayed late to clean up after the dance. How's Camille?"

"Just great," Sam spat. "How do you think she is?"

"Well, you don't have to be nasty. I didn't run her over." The wind threatened to pick up Kristine's hundred-dollar skirt. She pressed it against her legs. "I don't know who is nastier these days, you or your dear friend, Jen."

"Leave Jen out of this," Kenny defended.

Kristine snickered. "Jen is pretty out of it. From what I heard she was so out of it that she posed nude!"

Sam shot to her feet. Luckily they had rescued Jen before Jen had been photographed. And Jen had never wanted to pose for that horrible film. She'd been drugged and cleverly tricked into it by a sophisticated Hollywood scam. "She did not!"

Kristine backed up and waved her perfectly manicured nails. "Well, don't have a fit about it. I'm just repeating what I've heard around school." She looked back and forth between Sam and Kenny. "It's amazing what you can find out if you just keep your eyes and ears open."

Dylan stared at Kenny and Sam.

Now Kenny stood up, too, as if he were about to punch Kristine in her perfectly turned-up nose. But Kristine was already heading back to her little white Mustang.

"So glad we dropped by," Kristine said, giggling.

Dylan glared silently.

"And you know something, I don't think either of us will be dropping by again."

Sam felt the sudden sting of tears.

With that, Kristine opened her car door for Dylan and he climbed in. He didn't wave or look back as Kristine gunned her motor and sped away.

Coffee.

All Camille wanted on Sunday afternoon was a cup of coffee. Sweet, thick, dark espresso from her favorite hangout, Garo's Bookstore and Java House on Melrose Avenue.

"Why don't you just have plain steamed milk, Camille?" Sam suggested as they stepped out of Jen's mother's Nissan and blinked in the bright white sun. The Santa Ana winds had blown off, leaving stunningly clear skies and crisp desert air. It was one of those rare days when the mountains, usually hidden by smog, were visible in high relief.

"Garo makes a really good Italian soda," Jen added. She held out her hand to help Camille out of the car.

"I'm not a cripple," Camille barked. She brushed Jen's hand away, then watched the cars speed by. "I know I was just in the hospital, but

I'm okay now. I don't need help getting out of a car."

"Sorry," Jen whimpered. She turned away from Camille, then twisted her gauzy skirt as if she were wringing water out of it.

"I'm not mad at you," Camille backtracked. Why had she snapped at Jen? She knew that Jen was still feeling insecure—of course Jen, had always been insecure. As for herself, she had always been confident, so why was she suddenly feeling iffy. Of course, she *had* just gotten out of the hospital that morning. Even so, she muttered, "Sorry."

Jen chewed on the ends of her hair. "It's okay."

"Come on," cheered Sam, who clapped her hands like a Girl Scout troop leader. In fact, she looked like a Girl Scout in her khaki shorts and man's shirt. Of course, the Doc Martens and straw hat gave a whole other impression as she led the way past a sunglass boutique and a fancy flower shop.

They all glanced in Garo's front window, taking in the messy display of books and the bookstore cat, who was draped over a stack of fat Sunday newspapers.

"It's crowded," said Jen.

Camille stopped short in Garo's doorway, right between the anti-shoplifting device and the coterie of dogs that always hung out while their masters sipped and browsed. It *was* crowded. Stuffy, too, Camille noticed, as she bent down to pet a sleepy Irish setter. Feeling a little queasy, she took a deep breath, letting the dark espresso smell fill her lungs, her head, her soul. Oooh, the coffee smelled good. She'd only spent a day and two nights in the hospital, but she felt like she'd just completed a ten-year prison term. She never wanted to smell disinfectant or tomato soup again.

"Coffee," Camille moaned. "Give me coffee."

Jen nodded.

"Let's go!" Sam stomped past the first-floor bookstore customers, past potted plants that needed water, and up the old wooden stairs that squeaked with each step. The upstairs coffee-house was crowded, too, buzzing with mellow Sunday afternoon chatter. A new exhibit of paintings covered the whitewashed walls and Garo had just installed a computer so that customers could hook up to the Internet while they stoked themselves with caffeine.

Camille took a moment when she got to the top of the stairs. Suddenly everything was coming at her at once—the change in light, the thick smell, the bright colors, the beeping from the computer and the competing conversations. For a moment, she just concentrated on the sounds, which reminded her of an orchestra tuning up. Camille took in one flutelike chat about Melrose Avenue fashion, then tuned into a bass male voice arguing politics. But then the sounds collided in her ears and made her head ache again.

"Are you okay, Camille?" Sam asked as she stood on her tiptoes and looked around for a table.

Camille blinked. Now she felt as if the colors

weren't connected to the paintings, and the wooden ceiling beams clashed with the lights. It felt as if the coffeehouse had been broken down into separate pieces, each piece tied to a different sense and none of them quite fitting together.

"I must be tired," Camille admitted.

"Give me coffee," hooted Sam.

"JAVA," they chanted.

"There's a table," informed Jen.

They found seats in the corner. While Jen cleared the leftover Parcheesi pieces and a scattered newspaper, Camille slunk into an old captain's chair. She looked at preoccupied, delicate Jen, and at purposeful, quirky Sam and understood that she *was* tired. The doctor had forced her to spend that second night in the hospital, under observation. He'd wanted her to rest, too, which had seemed to Camille like a contradiction in terms. Her limbs had ached. The scrape on her face had throbbed, as if it had gotten deeper and more squished up. Besides that, how could she rest with the amount of noise and light that filled the hospital corridors? Not to mention what seemed like an hourly check on her vital signs. Camille had been woken up at least four times just to see if she was all right!

"Boy, am I glad to be back in the land of the living," Camille pronounced. She stretched her arms over her head, fluttering her fingernails, which she'd painted with stripes while lying in her hospital bed.

"And we're glad to have you back," Sam confirmed. "Although I did like watching Saturday morning cartoons with you yesterday. It was a truly eye-opening moment."

"Okay, I discovered that I have a weakness for Power Rangers," Camille joked. "Never again."

Sam sighed and waved her hands. "So who wants what to drink?"

Camille suddenly wanted to be jet-fueled. She wanted to feel normal, like the old unstoppable Camille again. "Double cappuccino," she ordered. "Fat milk. The fattest milk in the world."

Jen added a pig snort.

"Isn't that a little heavy duty?" Sam worried.

Camille made a face.

"How about single mochas?" Sam suggested.

"Okay," Camille gave in. "Semi-sweet."

"Extra whipped cream," Jen added.

Sam nodded and made her way to the counter.

Left alone with Jen, Camille started to feel better still. The noise and sound no longer clashed, and her headache disappeared. The only disconcerting thing now was Jen. Usually, Camille and Jen had an easy, big sister/little sister relationship. Camille always took the role of the elder, even though she was really younger by over eight months. She routinely gave sympathy, lectured, teased and sometime just plain forced advice down Jen's throat. Jen depended on her.

But today, Jen reacted to Camille with defensive eyes. She let her blond hair hide her face and scratched at sugar that had dried on the tabletop.

"Sam seems good," Camille mentioned.

Jen didn't agree. "She's kind of freaked about what happened with Dylan on Friday night. She figures this is it. He'll never talk to her again."

Camille shrugged. "He's just a guy."

Jen rolled her eyes, as if Camille were the most thick-headed boy-hater in West L.A.

"How was the hospital?" Jen finally asked.

Why had it taken Jen so long to mention Camille's accident? Camille had been hit by a car, and Jen was acting like she'd gotten a bad haircut. "What can I say? It wasn't a day at Disneyland. The CAT scan was pretty freaky. Luckily, I'm okay."

"Sorry I didn't visit you," Jen said softly. She wouldn't really look at Camille. "I couldn't get there. There was a problem with my mom's car."

"Oh well." Sam had spent most of Saturday with Camille, as had Camille's mom. Sam had told her all about Dylan catching her on the apartment stoop, until Kenny had showed up and the subject had been quickly dropped. Eventually Alison had stopped by, too, plus Camille's chem teacher and the entire debate team. It was odd that Jen hadn't visited, but Camille hadn't needed any more company. She reminded herself that Jen had always hated the sight of blood.

On the other hand, Camille had hated being

seen in that backless green smock. She'd loathed being fussed over and picked at. At least the CAT scan hadn't shown anything worrisome. In the end, the neurologist had just told Camille to take it easy. As long as Camille didn't experience any sudden seizures, vomiting, headache or vision problems, she was A-OK. After a little rest, life could go on as usual, which for Camille meant attacking everything one hundred and ten percent.

Camille touched the scrape on the side of her head. It was unbandaged, coated with yellow lotion. "Do I look really gross?"

Jen finally looked at Camille's wound, then quickly turned away, which only made Camille wonder if she looked even worse than she'd thought.

"A little makeup will cover it," Jen said.

Camille scoffed.

Jen shrugged. "Okay, so maybe it won't cover it up. It doesn't look that bad. It'll heal. Everybody knows what happened." Then Jen looked around, as if she didn't want anyone to hear her next question. "Um, so . . . do you remember what happened?" Jen asked in a tentative voice. "I mean, when you got hit?"

A folk/rock combo called West of Arizona, started to warm up near the back door and Camille was suddenly confused by the competing sounds again. "Not really. The police came and questioned me again. It wasn't Sam's mom this time. Or Carlos. It was some detective, this big guy who never smiled."

Jen fidgeted. "Were you able to tell him *anything*?"

Camille shook her head.

"You really don't know who hit you?"

"Nope."

"I wonder if they'll figure out who it was."

"Beats me."

Jen frowned, but Camille pretended not to care. In fact, she was very troubled by the fact that she couldn't remember anything about the accident. She knew that she'd seen the car. She had to have seen it. She even suspected that she'd seen the driver. But she couldn't recall any of the details. Why was that! Camille remembered the name of every kid in her first grade class. She memorized phone numbers after one calling. She was the mainstay of the Brain Bowl team, known for her recall of trivia. So why couldn't she remember something as big and obvious as one stupid automobile?

"Well, I guess it doesn't matter," Jen sighed. Her voice was a little shaky. "Maybe someone else saw the car."

Doesn't matter! Camille wanted to scream. What if that driver had killed her? What if that person had driven off and killed someone else? The driver had almost run her over, then sped off, as if he'd hit nothing more important than an empty cardboard box. Both Camille and the police had also wondered if the driver had been drunk.

Camille started to get angry at Jen's wimpiness. Sure, Jen had been through a humiliating experience, but Camille hadn't exactly been spending her last few days at an island resort. And she had an important three weeks coming up—maybe the most important three weeks in her entire life. Now she was going into it with a bruised body and the face of a prizefighter. "Luckily the Governor's Award doesn't give points for beauty."

"I'm sure you'll win," Jen murmured.

"I'm not," Camille snapped.

Jen sulked.

"Well, it won't be easy," Camille added. Again, she was aware of Jen taking offense. Sure, Camille had a good chance, but all six candidates were major contenders. Maybe that was Jen's problem. After losing the lead in the school play, Jen couldn't stand having Camille chalk up yet another accomplishment.

"Think of my competition," Camille couldn't help mentioning. "Barry, Suria. Kristine. Dylan and Rafe."

Jen rubbed her eyes.

"Rafe," Camille repeated silently. She suddenly wondered if she'd finally hit pay dirt. Could that be what was on Jen's mind? Rafe Danielson? Maybe Jen had really fallen for Rafe. They'd certainly looked cozy at the dance Friday night. Maybe Jen now felt that she had to support Rafe's candidacy instead of Camille's.

"How are things going with Rafe?" Camille dared to ask.

Jen smiled a little too quickly. "Great."

"Really?" Camille made sure. She didn't know

Rafe that well, since he'd only been at West L.A. High for a year.

"I like him a lot," Jen admitted.

Camille decided not to press the issue. Jen probably did feel caught between her and Rafe. "Well, all the finalists will have to work really hard. The winner will have to nail that American Values speech." She touched the scrape on her head. "Maybe I'll get some sympathy points."

There was another awkward pause, broken by Sam who had just wedged her way through the crowd, balancing three steaming mochas in tall, glass mugs. Sam handed them out and sat down. For a moment they all sipped and gulped. As soon as the dark sweetness hit Camille's stomach, she started to feel energized and hot.

"Sorry I took so long," Sam apologized. "I ran into . . ." Sam stopped her own train of thought, then pointed a finger. "Ick. Yuck. Ready or not, here she comes."

It was Dawn Warrington, dressed in her Sunday best—a frilly flowered skirt, blazer and old-fashioned high-button shoes. Her white blond hair was pinned up, with tiny ringlets corkscrewing down her cheeks and neck. Camille could imagine a little parasol twirling over her shoulder, except that Dawn was loaded down with a bag of newly purchased books, plus a take-out coffee.

"CAMILLE!" Dawn gushed. She squeezed her way over to the table. "I heard about what happened to you!"

"You seem to hear about everything, Dawn," Camille tossed back.

Dawn took a big breath. "I was sooo shocked. It must have awful. Who did it? Ew, look at your face. How are— "

Camille cut her off. "No need to ask. I'm fine. No one knows who hit me. I'm dandy."

Unable to look away from the scrape on Camille's face, Dawn wrinkled her nose.

Sam tapped Dawn's arm. "What's with all the books?"

Dawn readjusted herself. "I'm just picking up a few things up for Kristine Moore. Just some books for her American Values speech."

Yeah, like about ninety dollars worth, Camille wanted to point out. She wondered if Dawn might be working as research assistant, too. With relief, she remembered that Dawn wasn't the world's greatest student.

"Kristine's topic is Fairness and the Constitution," Dawn pronounced.

Fairness! If there was one thing Kristine *didn't* represent, it was fairness. Kristine had bought herself the lead in the school play—at Jennifer's expense! Fortunately, the Governor's Award couldn't be bought . . . at least Camille hoped that it couldn't.

"Who's writing the speech, Dawn?" Sam demanded. "Kristine or you?"

Dawn flinched. "Kristine. Of course."

"So why are you getting the books?" asked Jen.

"I'm just helping a friend. Kristine is really

busy, rehearsing for the play," Dawn answered pointedly. "They're having dress rehearsal all day today."

Jen shrunk back. She'd wanted that leading role so badly, and in fact had done a brilliant reading for it. But then Kristine's father had donated most of the money to renovate the school theater, and *surprise, surprise*, Kristine had been magically cast in the only female role.

Dawn locked onto Jen, obviously aware that she'd found a sore point. "The performances start soon. Thursday and Friday nights. And then again next Thursday and Friday. Are you all going to come?"

Jen pressed her hands to her eyes. Camille guessed that she was hiding sudden tears.

"We wouldn't miss it," Sam blurted.

"Well, don't," Dawn chirped. "No one should miss it." She checked her little bracelet watch. "Okay, I'd better go and get these to Kristine. I hope they figure out who hit you, Camille. Glad to see you up and about."

Camille considered throwing coffee at her.

Dawn ignored Camille's dirty looks. "Lots to do. So glad to run into you all. Camille, good luck with the Governor's Award. Ciao. Bye-bye. See you all at school tomorrow." With that, Dawn spun around and pranced down the stairs.

"She's really a pain, isn't she," Sam grumbled after Dawn had disappeared. "She and Kristine both. That whole social crowd makes me nuts. How could Dylan ever have hung out with them?"

Camille started to answer, then saw Jen lift her head. Her pale skin was blotchy and her makeup had run under one eye. She *had* been crying.

Sam touched Jen's hand.

Camille suddenly felt badly for Jen. She remembered just how much Jen had been through. Accident or no accident, Jen was one of her very best friends. "Don't worry, Jen. Kristine can't buy the Governor's Award. And she shouldn't have been allowed to buy that part in the school play!"

Jen chewed on her wooden stir stick. She managed a weak smile, even though her eyes had welled up again. "Thanks, Camille. I'm sorry I'm being so weird. I think I'm still getting over what happened to me. And I've been so worried about you."

Camille leaned her head, then flinched when she touched her scraped cheek to Jen's lacy shoulder. "Ow!"

"Sorry."

"It's not your fault."

"Oh, Camille," Jen sighed. "I'm so glad you're okay."

Finally they all laughed.

"Sorry I was so crabby," Camille said.

"Well, it's not like you haven't been through an awful lot," Jen confirmed. "It's okay."

"No, it's not," Camille stated in a loud voice. She pounded the table with her fist. "You've been through a lot, too, Jen. And now you're going to have to sit out in the audience and watch Kristine playing the lead in . . ." Camille stuttered.

Sam pounded the table, too, attempting to start a communal rhythm section. But Camille didn't react. She'd intended to mention the name of the play that Kristine would be appearing in, but the title just wouldn't come to her.

"The lead in . . . that play," Camille repeated. "You know, now we'll all have to go and watch Kristine parading around in . . . that play."

Jen nodded.

Sam raised her coffee cup.

Then Jen and Sam turned and starting jabbering with each other, deciding exactly which performance of the play they would attend and how they would keep themselves from throwing rotten fruit every time Kristine appeared on stage.

Meanwhile, Camille had started feeling pretty rotten, too. It was just the caffeine, she decided. Sam was right. Camille should never have drunk Garo's strong coffee after spending a day in the hospital, living on canned orange juice and mystery meat.

Camille's heart had begun to pound. Her forehead prickled with little beads of sweat. Her hands trembled and she couldn't quite catch her breath.

As Jen and Sam continued to chatter, Camille had to admit that it wasn't just the coffee that was getting to her. It was the fact that she couldn't remember . . . what was it . . . where had that little phrase gone? The title had something to do with weather, or making something, water, or Spain or clouds.

WHAT WERE THE WORDS! Where had they gone?

She never forgot things, Camille reminded herself. NEVER!

So why couldn't she remember the name of that stupid school play!

5

"*The Rainmaker*," Sam said to Jen.

"*The Rainmaker*," Jen echoed.

"And why is it called that? Why is *The Rainmaker* the title of this play?"

"Because, um, it's about this con man, this fake who says he can make it rain. See, it takes place in a farm town, and it hasn't rained in a long time . . . "

"So it's a drought. Like here in L.A."

"I guess. But this guy can't *really* make it rain . . . "

"So he's a phony."

"Sam, no one can really make it rain. Anyway, he just isn't what he says he is. But see, um, he makes Lizzy—she's this kind of old maid type who doesn't believe in herself, so he helps her have faith in herself, and that's real."

Sam settled into her theater seat and looked up at the dark semicircle of stage. It was the opening performance of *The Rainmaker*, the first West L.A. High production to be performed in the "New" Little Theater. Even though it was only a Thursday night, there seemed to be a good turnout.

"One thing we know for sure," Sam whispered. "Kristine Moore is a fake."

Jen clutched her stomach and groaned. "Don't remind me. This is going to be hard for me to watch."

Sam patted Jen's arm, then checked out the newly renovated West L.A. High Little Theater. Actually, the renovation—mostly paid for by Kristine's father—hadn't changed the theater's appearance very much. The seats were still covered with what looked like plaid carpeting. The rows were set in semicircles, and the few broken seats had been replaced by metal folding chairs. The thrust stage floor was still worn and dented. A painted snake still slithered along the back wall, even though most of its scales were chipping off.

Sam stowed her recycling bag under her seat and continued to look around. As Kristine's followers filed in, Jen hugged her notebook to her chest and chewed on her ballpoint pen. Sam figured that Kristine's spirit monsters would attend every performance. The clique numbered almost fifty. All wore new spirit outfits and expressions of great expectation as they filled the seats they saved for each other in the first few rows.

Sam shivered. The side door was open and

she could hear the wind kick up again. But it was a cool wind this time, one that made palm trees bend and doors slam unexpectedly. It had been windy like this when a small electrical fire had trashed the light board and caused the fire department to shut down the theater in the first place. But now the wiring had been redone, and new equipment has been purchased. The heating system kicked up the smell of sawdust and nervous anticipation.

"You okay?" Sam asked Jen.

Jen didn't look nervous. Of course, what was there for her to be nervous about? She already knew the outcome. Kristine had been cast, and Jen had been cast off.

"It's good that you came," Sam confirmed. "Maybe watching this will get it all out of your system."

Jen didn't look convinced. "Should we save a seat for Camille?"

Camille was another worry. Instead of taking it easy, Camille had been going full steam ahead since she got home from the hospital. "Camille's not coming," Sam informed. "She went to the Beverly Hills library, to do research for her Governor's Award Speech. Again. My mom still doesn't know who hit her. I think Camille wants to pretend it never happened."

Jen seemed relieved. "Rafe went to the West L.A. library to work on his speech, too." She smiled. "He's meeting me after the play."

Mentioning Rafe had made Sam think about Dylan and Kenny. Kenny had decided to skip the play, insisting that he would only pay *not* to watch Kristine Moore. And Sam had no idea whether Dylan might show up or not. She had no idea if he'd ever look at her again, for that matter. She'd tried to call him earlier in the week and he hadn't called her back, so she knew he wasn't speaking to her. Since then, she hadn't run into him at school.

Sam knelt on her seat for a while, facing the back of the auditorium while the crowd continued to file in. She waved to friends from Club, Club and a fellow youth center volunteer. Just when the lights started to fade, she spotted Dylan. He was with two other juniors from track—they looked like twins in their identical team sweatshirts. In contrast, Dylan's shirt advertised the Santa Monica Airport, which made Sam remember how he had once told her of his love for airplanes and his desire to learn to fly. Dylan looked sad, even preoccupied and Sam suddenly felt sad, too. She popped up in her seat and waved.

"Dylan!" she called out.

Dylan saw her. He had to have seen her. Everybody in the back of the theater could see her, especially now that she was bobbing up and down like an idiot. In fact, Sam saw Dylan focus right on her face, then rearrange his perception, turning her into empty air.

Oh, come on, Sam wanted to yell. *Dylan!* She was suddenly furious. Why couldn't they talk and at least be friends? If they'd really had something great together—which for a few fleeting moments they'd had—did it all have to all fall apart because of one kiss? Couldn't she feel strongly about Kenny, and feel the same way about Dylan at the same time?

Unfortunately, Sam knew the answer.

No way.

Sam could feel any way she wanted, and so could Dylan. But what Dylan was feeling right now was anger and possibly a desire to erase Sam from the face of the planet. Sam wondered if she would have reacted the same way, then decided that she wouldn't have. Not with Dylan. Not with anyone she really cared about. Not ever!

Embarrassed and hurt, Sam sunk back down. The lights were starting to dim. Jen had set her notebook on her lap and was doodling madly as the audience went dark and the lights came up on the stage. The stage set was minimal—a fence, the outline of a weathervane, benches, tables and horse tack. A senior strummed a guitar on the side as the play began with the male characters discussing the drought and worrying about what they were going to do.

Then Sam heard a little groan and realized that it had come from Jen. Sam looked up at the stage again and saw that Kristine had made her entrance. Kristine looked beautiful. Her golden hair, rolled into ringlets, glittered in the stage light. Her perfect skin glowed. Even her plain dress had obviously been bought at some expensive costume house, while the other clothes had been pulled from the school's dusty collection, then combined with modern vests and Levi's. No hand-me-downs for Kristine. She looked magazine-cover elegant, as she gracefully strolled across the stage.

Then Sam remembered that Kristine's character, Lizzy, was supposed to be homely and plain. Now Sam felt as angry and frustrated as Jen. She cringed as Kristine took center stage and prepared for her first big speech. Kristine's groupies were pitched forward as if they were watching Meryl Streep. Kristine opened her beautiful mouth, and out came a sound that was at once shocking and laughable.

"Hi, boys," Kristine whined.

Kristine was attempting a midwestern accent, but she sounded like she was speaking a combination of valley girl twang and off-key Chinese. Her hands were balled up in nervous little fists. Even her spiffy pioneer wear couldn't disguise the tension that contorted her chest. Then she had a moment of panic where she'd obviously forgotten a line. The freshman boy who played her little brother came in and saved her.

"She's so awful!" Sam whispered to Jen.

Jen just kept doodling.

The more Sam watched, the more angry she became. Pretty soon, the absurdity of it all started to make her feel woozy. Jen had been the best actress, but rich Kristine had been given the part. Kenny had been her best friend, and now Dylan was distant and jealous. None of it made any sense!

Sam figured she had two choices as she continued to watch *The Rainmaker*. She could laugh or scream. Knowing that a scream would probably get her kicked out of school, she started to giggle. The more she tried to hold her laughter back, the funnier and more ridiculous it seemed.

"SHHHHHHH!" ordered Stacy DeFonte, another of Kristine's groupies.

Sam finally had to clap her hand over her mouth, to keep herself from screaming *and* laughing. Someone tapped her shoulder from behind, then pointed to Dawn Warrington, who shot Sam a furious look. That only made Sam want to laugh harder. In fact, the more Kristine emoted, the more Sam's shoulders shook and her stomach ached.

"I can't stand this," she panted.

Luckily, just then, the freshman who played Kristine's little brother did a funny bit of business and the whole audience enjoyed a laugh, too. Sam was finally able to release some of her absurd feelings and laugh out loud.

"AGHHHHHHHHH!"

Sam laughed. She gasped and guffawed and fell over her knees until the energy sputtered out of her.

"This is too much," she stammered.

But then she looked over at Jen again and she didn't feel like laughing any more.

Jen wasn't amused at all. Not by Kristine, or Sam, or the freshman making goofy faces and turning somersaults on stage. The only thing Jen was doing was staring down at a cartoon she'd drawn of Kristine Moore. Holding her pen like a knife, Jen was poking holes all over Kristine's face, until Kristine's image was nothing but violent stabs and shreds.

Jen bolted out during the curtain call.

Even though people were still clapping, she hobbled along the row of seats, stomping over books and on top of feet. When Kristine came out for her bow, Jen rudely sped up her exit and plowed her way up the aisle.

"Jen," Sam whispered.

She wasn't sure what to do. Should she follow? Should she wait? Jen had created quite a disturbance, and she'd also left her Western Civ books under her chair. Sam gathered up Jen's things, and in the process kicked her own bag over, spilling pen, makeup and keys.

Stacy DeFonte actually kicked the back of Sam's chair as Sam scrambled to collect her stuff. Sam got the message. She decided to hold tight until the curtain call was finished. Sam and Jen were already on that social crowd's hit list. There was no point in making things even worse.

Towards that end, Sam applauded for Kristine. Then she waited patiently as everyone trudged up and out. She looked around for Dylan, then felt angry all over again when she couldn't find him this time. When she reached the foyer, she didn't see Jen either. She saw Kristine's social toadies all standing around, congratulating themselves. Even so, they didn't stick around for long, and Sam had the feeling that even they knew that their fearless leader had come up short.

Sam stood around, trying not to attract the attention of the social crowd and wondering just what had happened to Jen. Jen had been acting so weird lately. Sam wondered if Jen had just run off, even though she would have to walk two miles in the dark to get home.

"Jen . . . JEN!"

Sam walked up and down the hallway, past the library and the janitor's closet. She walked all the way down past the glass trophy case, then walked faster when she noticed some track trophies engraved to both Dylan and Rafe Danielson. She took one last glance and realized that the hallway had totally cleared out. She was about to clear out, too, when she jogged back past the library and saw Jen flop down until she was sitting cross-legged on the floor.

Jen hugged her notebook to her chest. Her eyes were red. She looked grim.

"There you are," Sam said. "I couldn't find you."

"I couldn't stand it," Jen moaned.

"I know. Kristine was awful. It's not fair, but at least it's over. I'm not in a great mood either," Sam admitted. "Let's go home."

Jen didn't budge and Sam finally remembered that Jen was supposed to meet Rafe. Rafe was nowhere in sight. "Are you still meeting Rafe?"

Jen shook her head, then pulled a folded piece of paper out of her patchwork purse. "He left a note in my locker. That's where I was. I went upstairs to get a book out of my locker, and I found his note. Rafe had to cancel tonight, because he has so much studying to do."

"Well, it is a weeknight." Sam had studying of her own, she remembered, as well as an early weeknight curfew. She headed for the exit.

Jen slowly got up. "Rafe's calling me later." She slipped the note back into her purse. "We'll go out this weekend. He wants to go roller skating at this rink in Hollywood."

"Maybe Kenny and I will go, too." Sam held the door open for Jen.

Jen was moving like she was in slow motion. Finally she joined Sam in the doorway. Sam handed Jen her Civ books. "Come on."

They trudged across the parking lot in silence. The light was still broken near where Camille had been hit, and this time Sam was glad that it was so dark. She didn't want to look at Jen's hurt face. She didn't want to think about how unfair the play had been, or how Dylan wouldn't even look at her.

They still hadn't said a word when they reached Sam's mom's car. With a yawn, Sam dug in her bag. Then she was hit with a shot of adrenaline. She dug and dug.

Where were her car keys?

Sam checked her pockets. She emptied her bag out and searched her wallet.

"What's up?" Jen asked.

"Darn!" Sam grunted. "My mom's car keys must have fallen out of my bag. I must have left them in the theater." She looked around. There were no other cars in the parking lot.

Jen looked around, too.

"I guess I'll have to call my mom," Sam decided. Then remembered that her mom was on shift. That meant calling the station and having them patch Sam through to the patrol car. It also meant riding home in an LAPD black-and-white. On second thought, maybe Sam would call Kenny. He could hop on his motor scooter and bring them a spare key.

Jen thought for a minute, then put her hand on Sam's arm. "Look, we can get back into the theater from the back door, where the dressing rooms are."

"It'll be locked."

Jen rolled her eyes. "The door there can be jiggled open, unless they just fixed it." She sighed. "We used to sneak in there last fall to rehearse on weekends. It's no big deal."

Of course, Jen knew every inch of the theater building. Before the electrical fire, she'd taken drama class in there and she'd been in three productions. Even so, Sam felt uneasy. She knew that her mom had busted kids for trespassing on school property at night. Of course, she and Jen weren't really trespassing, she told herself. They were just going back in to collect her keys.

Jen was already leading the way back across the dark parking lot. Telling herself that she had no choice, Sam followed.

Jen walked straight to the theater back door. Sure enough, she jiggled the lock, then popped it open with her ballpoint pen. Without looking, she tapped the light switch.

Sam stepped in, too. They headed down some concrete steps, and into a narrow, plain hall.

"We just pass the dressing rooms, then go up the stairs and we'll be on the stage." Jen said. "Then we just climb down and find your keys."

"I hope you know where the lights are in there," Sam prayed.

But Jen didn't respond. She'd stopped at the dressing room doorway and flicked on the light switch. She let out a loud sigh.

"Will you look at this?" Jen demanded.

Sam backed up and peeked in. The Little Theater's dressing room was just a ten foot corridor with a concrete floor, counters on either side and eight individual mirrors. Each mirror had been assigned to an actor and marked with a three by five card.

Sam didn't need to read the cards to locate Kristine's dressing space. While other spaces held lonely tubes of Maybelline, a box of Kleenex, bottle of white shoe polish, or a few good luck cards, Kristine's space had a huge, professional-looking makeup box, left open and filled with Clinique and Estée Lauder. Good luck gifts abounded—ribbons and hearts, joke rain detectors, tiny horses and china cows. There was a set of electric rollers, plus a curling iron. Most impressive was the bouquet of flowers that overflowed onto the next space.

Jen couldn't resist stepping over and reading the florist's card. *"To my brilliant, talented daughter,"* Jen read out loud. *"I am so proud of you. You deserve this honor. You are the shining star of West L.A. High. There will never be a drought in my love for you. Daddy."*

Just reading a greeting card, Jen was a better actress than Kristine. Sam began to feel so angry again. She felt like picking up the bouquet of flowers and throwing it all over the stage.

Jen was obviously feeling the same way. Her face was flushed. She bit her lip and hugged her slim body, as if she were fighting violent impulses, too.

"Sick," Jen finally commented.

"It is sick," Sam confirmed. She also knew that Jen's father would never dream of writing a note like that. Jen's father belittled Jen's desire to become an actress. He always told her to stop being overdramatic, then pointed out all of her shortcomings.

Sam ranted, "Sick. Gross. Unfair. Wrong, wrong, wrong!"

"I KNOW!" Jen screamed. "That part was mine. It should have been mine. Why did this happen?" Then she began to cry. These were no held-back trickles. Jen had begun to wail and sob.

Even as Sam hugged Jen, she had an eerie feeling. It was always eerie to be on campus when no one else was around, especially after dark. Sam just wanted to do something . . . anything . . . to ease Jen's pain. Not knowing what else to do, she left Jen and picked up the bouquet of flowers. "Don't tell anyone," Sam made Jen promise.

Jen sniffled and watched her.

Knowing that she was being stupid and immature, Sam took the flowers over to the sink, emptied the water, then put the blossoms back in the vase. She placed the vase back on Kristine's counter. "Dry up and wither, Daddy's girl. Phony. Show your true colors."

Jen couldn't help smiling.

Sam gave a triumphant gesture and started to head for the door. Then she realized that Jen wasn't joining her. Jen was stuck at Kristine's dressing space. To Sam's amazement, Jen was unzipping her own shoulder bag. She pulled out a tiny vodka bottle, the kind they gave out on airplanes. With a flourish, she twisted off the top, then began to drink.

"Jen!" Sam gasped. "Where did you get that?"

"I just stole it from my parents liquor cabinet. I've never done it before. I figured I might need a little help getting through tonight. You want some?" She shivered as she took another swig.

"NO."

Jen shrugged, then took a lipstick out of Kristine's makeup box and unrolled it. Then she leaned toward Kristine's mirror. *SICK*, Jen stabbed out in brownish-red letters.

"Jen!" Sam objected.

Jen didn't listen. She threw the lipstick on

the counter and took up an eyebrow pencil. With a faint sputter, she scrawled, *PHONY.*

"Jen!"

Jen's face had taken on a hard, obsessed look. She tossed the eyebrow pencil and grabbed a fat, blue shadow crayon. She scribbled, *NO TALENT.*

Sam was appalled. She hated drinking. She hated being stupid and cruel. And yet a little part of her understood, too. How was Jen supposed to feel? And what was she supposed to do about it? School was supposed to be fair. Honors were supposed to be given to those who deserved them, those who had displayed talent and hard work.

Sam rushed over to stop Jen from doing any further damage. Jen finished the vodka, then stowed the bottle back in her purse.

Sam looked for some paper towels to clean the mirror. But then she looked at Jen and realized that everything Jen had written was true. She picked up a pink lipstick and added to the graffiti. *BUY, BUY, BUY,* she wrote, her arm flailing so wildly that her earring swung hard against her cheek.

Jen started to laugh. She took the lipstick out of Sam's hand, then drew wild circles, faces, zigzags and lines.

WANT, WANT. GET, GET. HAVE, HAVE, Sam added.

DADDY'S GIRL, Jen stabbed out. Then Jen raised her hand to add one last streak of color. As she brought her hand down, she accidentally whacked the glass vase of flowers.

CRAAAAASSSSSSSHHHHH!

Sam gasped.

The noise was terrifying. Shards of glass shot everywhere. Flowers scattered. Sam leapt back, dropping Kristine's eyeliner brush. Jen cowered, too.

For a moment both of them stood in terrified silence.

"Let's get out of here," Sam gasped.

"Let's go," confirmed Jen.

Sam's heart throbbed as she led the way into the dark theater. Jen didn't find the light this time. On her hands and knees, Sam crawled alone the floor, between the seats.

"I found the keys!" Jen gasped in slurry voice.

Sam fell over chairs and almost stumbled up the steps. Somehow she and Jen made it out of the dark theater. They ran across the parking lot and didn't breathe again until they were safely locked inside Sam's mother's car.

6

It didn't feel any better.

It was supposed to even the score, to stop the silence and make them see me again.

LOOK. LOOK. Talk to me. Don't act like I'm not here!

What would it take to make them notice. What would it take to make them pay respect. What would it take to make them really care?

It was another quiet Friday night on the streets of West L.A.

With the exception of Camille's accident, nothing remarkable had taken place for two whole weeks. Alison and Carlos had been called in as back-up for a Laurel Canyon drug bust. Then they'd sat in their car, while the Narcotics Squad had handled everything. They'd been called in on an armed robbery, too, except that the action was all over by the time they'd arrived. Then there'd been the usual array of minor teen problems—loitering, shoplifting, just plain acting like a jerk. Most serious had been a psychotic freak-out from a youth center runaway, and a kid who'd pulled a knife on someone who hadn't liked the color of his shoes.

Alison sat in the front seat of the squad car while Carlos drove. "The exciting life of a rookie cop," she sighed.

"Don't complain," joked Carlos. "You want more action, let them send you downtown."

"Okay, okay."

Alison chuckled, then turned serious again. Of course, there was also Camille's hit-and-run. No one took Camille's accident lightly. Camille seemed to be okay, but Alison was frustrated that they had come up with no leads as to the identity of the driver.

So far, they had no witnesses.

No clues.

Nada.

Alison checked her watch. "Let's get this show on the road."

Carlos nodded. They were driving past the back of West L.A. High. He parked, so that they could walk the neighborhood and see if they could find any witnesses for the hit-and-run. Alison craned her neck to look on to campus. Sam had gone back to school that night to see the play. Most of the campus lights were off, though. The school play was obviously over.

"Sam must be home by now, or on her way," Alison mentioned. "I don't like her being home alone at night." She rearranged her holster, which was well-hidden under a baggy wool blazer. Then she climbed out of the black-and-white.

"Don't rush me," Carlos bantered. He hiked up his own weapon, which was slung around the waist of his LAPD blues. Popping a stick of Juicy Fruit in his mouth, he locked up the car. "We haven't exactly made progress on this hit-and-run case, and right now it's the slimiest offense on our plate."

Alison glanced down Bonita, and then along Orange. The cool breeze made her shiver.

Carlos, who had an uncanny ability to spot important things in the landscape, pointed down towards the middle of the block. "Well, well. I think the Carellis are finally home. We haven't talked to them in a while."

Alison glanced down Orange Street, too. Sure enough, there were lights on in the small, rundown house where Mr. and Mrs. Carelli lived with three dogs and their fourteen-year-old son, Randy.

Alison began to stroll. Half a block later she could hear rock music blaring from the Carelli house. "No one was home at the Carelli's the night of the accident," she reminded Carlos. "I still haven't interviewed Randy or the parents. What do you think?"

"It's a long shot." Carlos shrugged as he walked faster. "But they could have seen something from their window. If they'd been looking."

"It's been a while since we've checked up on them anyway," Alison decided.

"Can't hurt."

Carlos led the way past three more small bungalows with patchy lawns and rusty cars. During the weekend following Camille's accident, Carlos and Alison had interviewed almost everyone who could have seen the car plow into Camille. No one had seen a thing. The only people they'd been unable to reach so far had been the oh-too-familiar Carelli family.

Alison stopped in front of the Carelli house. The music was some kind of acid rock, ear-shatteringly loud. Out front was a bricked-off flower bed that contained only dirt and chewed-up dog toys. The garage was open and displayed a mess of tools, boxes, dog beds, a hunting rifle, old lumber plus a washing machine surrounded by dirty laundry. Of course, none of the houses on Orange Street were exactly manicured mansions. Being across the street from a large public high school wasn't exactly a desirable locale.

Even so, the Carellis had a special distinction for the LAPD. Mr. Carelli had a tendency for beating up on Mrs. Carelli, Randy, even their three large dogs—basically anyone who interfered with his alcoholic rages. Alison had only shown up once for a domestic violence call. Carlos had been there many times. Randy had already chalked up arrests for stealing CDs, buying booze with a false ID, and throwing bottles at passing cars.

Alison surveyed the house. The living room was brightly lit, but she didn't see anyone. "I still think that someone was home here the night of Camille's accident. I think they just didn't want to open the door to us. Either they'd been fighting, or they were just trying to sleep."

"Or they just didn't want to see our ugly faces again." Carlos smiled.

"That, too."

Carlos marched up the broken concrete path and pounded on the Carelli's screen door. "HELLO!" he called over the blasting music. "MRS. CARELLI! MR. CARELLI, IT'S OFFICER CARLOS."

Alison pressed the doorbell. She pressed again. The music was so loud that she couldn't tell if the bell was even working.

Finally they sensed the padding of feet on the other side of the door.

"WHO IS IT?" a young male voice asked.

Alison cupped her hands around her mouth. "IT'S OFFICER CRANE. RANDY? IT'S ALISON AND CARLOS."

The door opened very slowly. On the other side of the screen stood fourteen-year-old Randy, wearing gray cut-off sweats and a blocky plaid shirt. He was almost six feet tall, but quite thin, with pale pimpled skin. A bandanna was tied over his hair and his skinny feet were bare. From the thumping of the music, Alison had expected to see a party inside. But she only saw Randy.

"RANDY," Carlos hollered. He smiled with his best macho warmth. "CAN WE COME IN?"

"What for?" Randy mumbled. "I didn't do nothin.'"

"We didn't say you did," Alison soothed. "We just wanted to check in on you, to see if you were all right."

Randy glared. A big, mangy collie dog came up and nuzzled his leg. Finally, Randy opened the door. The collie almost slithered out. While Randy grabbed him, Carlos and Alison walked into the living room.

The music was so loud inside that it hurt Alison's ears. The living room consisted of two old couches, a tree trunk coffee table, a dog bed, stained shag carpet and a messy TV/stereo/computer entertainment center. Every inch of living room had been scratched and chewed by the dogs.

Carlos went right to the stereo. He put his hand on the volume knob. "DO YOU MIND?"

Randy slunk onto the sofa. Two other dogs came in. One was a pit bull, the other some kind of Shepherd mix. The dogs bounded around the room like they'd been jet-fueled.

Carlos turned off the music.

Randy sulked.

"Where are your folks?" Carlos asked in a friendly voice.

"Out."

"Out where?" Carlos asked.

"My mom's working. I don't know about my dad."

Alison smiled. "How is your mom? Is your dad still living here?"

Randy hugged the pit bull.

Alison reminded herself that Randy was only fourteen. How many nights did he spend here all by himself? She sat on the tree trunk table so that she faced him directly. "How's it been going?"

"How's what going?" Randy mumbled.

"How's it going with your dad? Has it gotten any better? Is he still drinking as much?"

"What do you think?" Randy shot back.

Alison touched his hand.

Surprisingly, he didn't flinch.

"Randy, you know that if it gets bad and you need a place to go, or your mom does, you can call me or Carlos." Alison handed him a card with the station phone number. "We can find you another place to stay if you're in danger. There are shelters—"

"I can take care of my mom!" Randy interrupted proudly.

For a moment no one said anything.

The collie barked.

"We know you can take care of your mom," Carlos finally said. "We just want to help."

Randy rolled his eyes and Alison knew that Carlos was on the wrong track. "Randy, how's school?" she asked casually. She found it hard to imagine Randy in the same school with kids like Samantha, Jen and Camille. Nevertheless, he was a freshman at West L.A. High—unless he'd dropped out.

He gave a shrug and glared at Carlos. When Randy wasn't looking, Alison gestured for Carlos to give her and Randy some space. Picking up her cue, Carlos wandered. He parked himself just outside the screen door.

Randy seemed to relax as soon as Carlos was out of the room. "School is okay. Some of it," he admitted.

"What parts are okay?" Alison pressed. This was where she was most comfortable, just dealing with kids in a one-to-one situation.

"Not English, that's sure."

Alison nodded. "English is hard?"

"English is stupid."

"Luckily, high school isn't just English."

He glanced up, then hugged the dog again. "Computer class isn't bad," he muttered.

"Really?" She'd noticed the computer equipment in the entertainment center. It was all mismatched and outdated. Nevertheless, it all looked well-used and tweaked to some specific purpose. "Is that your stuff?"

He glanced at the computer. "Maybe. Some of it."

"Could you show it to me?"

After a pause, he shuffled over and flipped on the screen. The mere fact that he collected it all and made it work was pretty impressive. He shoved in a disk, then keyed up some graphics. They were what looked like original artwork of unusual superheroes. He'd managed to make his heroes move, even fight.

"What is this, Randy?"

"Just some of my designs."

"Your designs?" Alison made sure. "You did this? You mean, designed this?"

Randy stared at the screen. Finally he nodded.

"Randy, this is great. You're really good at this."

He seemed embarrassed, but pleased. "That's what my mom says."

"She's right."

Randy tried not to smile.

"Randy, are you enrolled in any programming classes at school?"

He didn't answer.

"Maybe I can find out about some special computer art programs at West L.A. High. Or at the junior college. You're a freshman now, right?"

Randy looked dubious.

"It doesn't matter. I'll find out and let you know."

Just then, Carlos came back into the room. Randy immediately turned off his computer. Carlos gestured to his watch. Alison remembered Sam and the fact that her shift was almost over.

"Thanks for showing me that, Randy," she managed. "I meant what I said. I'll find out all I can."

Randy was about to say something, but Carlos didn't want to waste any more time. "Look, Randy," he stated, "last Friday night, there was a hit-and-run accident right in front of your house. Did you see anything?"

Randy seemed confused. And scared. "What time?"

"A little before nine," Alison answered.

Randy backed away. "I was with my friend Fred Gomez," he swore. "You can call him." He picked up the phone and thrust it at Carlos.

Alison tried to calm him. "You're not a suspect, Randy. We wanted to know if you might have seen the car. We're looking for witnesses."

"I wasn't home," Randy said.

"How about your mom?"

"Or your dad?" Carlos blurted.

Randy looked angry now. "I don't know. Ask him."

Alison walked up to Randy and put her hand on his arm again. "We'll go now, Randy. Thanks for letting us in."

They started to leave, but Randy stopped them at the door. "Officer Crane. If you do find out about any computer design things, you let me know. You won't forget, will you?"

"I won't forget, Randy."

"Okay."

Alison led the way back to the squad car. She and Carlos rode in silence, all the way back to Spaulding. Carlos was dropping her off, since she'd given Sam her car for the evening.

When Carlos turned onto Spaulding, he finally said, "He was like a different kid."

"Who?"

"Randy. I was listening when you were in there alone with him. With you, he was like a different kid."

"Maybe he's the real Randy with me," Alison came back.

Carlos pulled into the alley next to her building. He let out a loud sigh. "Maybe he is."

* * *

Alison was feeling cocky when Carlos dropped her off at her apartment. Carlos was right. Randy had been different with her. She'd managed to zero in on what was positive in Randy, what was hopeful and might pull him through. If she could just find a way to do that with more kids, maybe she'd know exactly what to propose to her sergeant. Maybe she could make a difference with every teen in L.A.

"Randy, Randy." Alison smiled as she stepped over a Frisbee and strolled across the apartment lawn.

Then she stopped. Maybe she was feeling too cocky, because she almost hadn't spotted Samantha, who had just parked the car in their space behind the apartment. And maybe there was a difference between dealing with someone else's kid and coping with your own. Sam spotted Alison, then tried to slink in the dark, as if she didn't want to be seen.

Alison didn't let Sam off the hook. She stepped into the light and called, "Sam, why are you so late getting home?"

Sam seemed tired and grumpy. She also seemed to want to avoid Alison. "Jen and I went to the play."

"I know you went to the play."

Sam hurried past Alison, not quite looking at her.

All of Alison's confidence fell flat. Was Sam in a snit over Dylan? Was this about a test, a fight with a teacher, a misunderstanding with Kenny? Was Sam coming down with the flu?

Alison caught up with Sam near the apartment garbage cans. "The play was over by ten fifteen. I was just over near campus. The school was all dark."

"Oh." Sam kicked an empty paper cup that had been blown out of the trash can. "So?"

She sensed that Sam was avoiding something. "Sam, don't just kick that. Pick it up." She instantly regretting nagging Sam about something so lame. But she hated it when Sam avoided her and acted sullen. "Sorry," she backtracked. "What's going on, Sam. Are you okay?"

Sam strode along the alley and Alison followed. When Alison caught up to Sam, Sam muttered, "I had to drive Jen home. We stopped to talk for a while."

"How's Jen doing?"

"Fine," Sam snapped. "And oh, I dropped the car keys. Before I drove Jen home, I mean. So I had to go back into school to get them. That's why I'm late."

"Oh."

Sam tossed Alison the keys, but still wouldn't look at her. Then they passed Kenny's kitchen window. The light was on and Alison could hear Kenny practicing his guitar. Alison waved to Kenny's father's girlfriend, who was pulling something out of the oven.

Sam just stormed past. Usually Sam couldn't pass Kenny's window without stopping to tease, or offering come kind of crack.

Sam hurried to the apartment front door.

She let it slam just as Trash Man, the alley cat, squirted through.

"Sam!" Alison warned.

"What?"

"You almost closed the door on Trash Man. Look what you're doing!"

Ignoring her mother, Sam plowed into the lobby. Trash Man scampered up the stairs ahead of them. Alison stopped to collect the mail. She watched Sam race up the stairs.

Loaded down with catalogues and bills, Alison met Sam at their apartment door. "Sam, what is going on? Do you feel okay? Did something happen tonight?" Alison unlocked their door.

"I'm just tired," Sam murmured. She slid past Alison, dropped her books in the foyer and headed straight for her room.

Alison knew something was up. Sam had her moods and her tantrums. But she was rarely like this. Alison knocked on Sam's door. "Sam. Sam!"

"What?"

"Sam, can I come in? You're obviously upset about something. Why don't we talk about it."

Alison waited. She stood in the hall for what seemed like ten minutes. Traffic wafted by. The refrigerator cycled.

Finally Sam opened her door. She'd changed into a sloppy UCLA nightshirt that she'd permanently borrowed from Alison. She hadn't washed off her eye makeup and the long earring that Jen had made for her in art class was broken.

The hand-painted bead was gone, so that Sam was wearing only a dangly, limp chain.

Sam just stared down at the floor.

Alison knew that Sam wasn't going to open up right away. She decided to break the ice by changing the subject. "Sam, I had a pretty interesting evening. Want to hear about it?"

Sam shrugged.

Alison barged ahead, still standing in the doorway. "Okay. I talked to this kid who lives right near school. I'm sure you don't know him, but seeing him tonight gave me an idea."

Sam just stood there.

"I'm starting to think about ideas to propose to the sergeant, about new ways of dealing with juvenile crime. I've been thinking about how much time I have to spend away from you, and how West L.A. High seems to be a good place to start."

Sam lifted her face. She looked doubtful.

"I thought I'd start a program that I'd try out first at West L.A. High."

Sam took a deep breath.

Alison was prepared to explain her ideas to Sam, to present the reason why she thought her program was important and how Sam could even get involved. Then she hoped that eventually Sam would relax and explain why she was in such a lousy mood. But instead, Sam just said, "Do whatever you want." Then she whispered good night, turned around and closed her door.

Alison stood in the hall for what felt like another ten minutes. Finally she padded into the living room and turned on the TV. Staring at the evening news, she stretched out her legs and hugged her middle.

That night she'd felt like the best cop in Los Angeles. And the city's worst mom.

7

"You were so wonderful in the play last night, baby."

"I was not, Dad."

"Krissie, how can you say that? I was so proud of you. You were perfect."

Kristine Moore sat stone-faced.

"Don't be sad, honey. Please. Come on. How about if we go shopping tomorrow? Your mother's working. We could hit Rodeo Drive and have a blast. What do you say?"

"I don't say, 'have a blast,' Dad. In my whole life, I've never said, 'have a blast.'"

"I'm sorry, Krissie."

"Forget it, Dad. Thanks for the ride. See you later."

"I'll be at your play again tonight, honey. You know I will."

"Please don't come *again*, Dad."

"Why not?"

"It's embarrassing."

He looked hurt. "Do you have your outline for your Governor's Award Speech?"

"Of course I have it, Dad!"

"I know you'll win that award, honey."

"Yeah, right," Kristine Moore muttered as she slammed the door of her father's Mercedes and pretended that he was no longer there. Even so, her dad hung around as long as he could. His fat, shiny face beamed at her over the steering wheel. Finally he pulled his car along the circular drive, past the flagpole and the teachers' parking lot. Kristine stood at the bottom of the school front steps, not moving until his personalized DR FACE license plate disappeared from view.

Then she took a deep breath and squinted in the bright sun. She smelled the perfume her mom had brought for her from Paris. She was aware of her blond hair falling gracefully to her shoulder, the imported cotton against her skin, the tooled leather boots stiff and tight around her calves. She knew she looked older than seventeen and wondered if anyone would hassle her if she left campus and cut school.

But then she remembered that her Mustang was in the shop—it was finally being detailed after an angry, lowlife girl had stubbed out a cigarette on the sparkling white hood. That's why her dad had needed to drive her to school.

Besides that, she would never cut. And she wouldn't give up. Not Kristine Moore. She'd been trained since babyhood. The best preschools, private El Rancho Elementary, then St. Mary's for middle school. She'd begged and pleaded to be able to finally attend public West L.A. High. She'd finally convinced her father, and she wasn't about to blow it over something as small as this.

Except that this was no small thing, she told herself as she trudged up the front steps, away from the sprinklers that sent fresh rainbows across the school's front lawn. Kristine only wished that she could feel that sparkly and fresh. Maybe if her father just backed off for a while, she'd feel better. Maybe if he'd just leave her alone, she'd start to relax.

Kristine pushed open the double doors at the front of the school, ducking under a spirit banner that she'd tacked up herself. It wasn't that her father pressured her, like the parents of other L.A. kids she'd knew. He just thought that she was perfect. And if there was anything *unperfect* about her, well, he'd just pay to have it fixed. Maybe that's why he had become a plastic surgeon. He was a lumpy, plain man who couldn't believe he'd sired such a pretty daughter. He idolized beauty. Transforming his rich patients gave him great joy. His patients considered him a magician, and paid him handsomely to revamp their faces and bodies, their marriages and their careers.

"Don't think about it," Kristine told herself. "Just drop off your outline for the Governor's Award, then deal with this day."

That was one more thing nagging at her. The

Governor's Award. She'd arrived early to turn in her speech outline to the vice principal, even though she didn't want to think about Fairness and the Constitution. If it hadn't been for her father's beaming confidence in her, she never would have entered the contest. Between the spirit activities, the play and the scores of so-called friends who hung all over her, she was already on overload.

She turned and walked into the principal's office just as Suria Lu was walking out. Super competitive Suria, looking sleek and wide shouldered in her swim team sweats, wouldn't even meet Kristine's eye.

So Kristine turned up her nose, too, and approached the counter. "Here's my speech outline for the Governor's Award," she told the secretary, a sweet older woman named Mrs. Guitierez. All the kids called her Goots.

"I'm coming to your play tonight," Goots said grinning. She took Kristine's outline and placed it in a special folder. "I heard you all were just wonderful."

Kristine couldn't manage a smile. She knew that she'd stunk up the place as Lizzie the previous night. For the last two weeks of rehearsal she'd known that she was no actress. Even so, she'd never dreamed that she'd freeze as badly as she had on her opening night. When she'd heard the rustle of the crowd, she'd almost thrown up. The sight of her admirers had made her limbs shake and her stomach cramp up. Then she'd heard that vicious Samantha Crane giggling and she'd stopped breathing. Time had stretched out endlessly. Kristine had wanted nothing more than to be lifted off the stage and beamed far away from southern California. But she'd never been a quitter, and she wasn't going to start becoming one now.

"Samantha," Kristine grumbled as she left the office and wandered back into the hall. She held her head high, intimidating the other early birds that were rushing into the library or staring into their lockers. How dare Sam laugh at her like that! If Jen had been playing the part, Kristine would never have laughed! Samantha was always putting Kristine down, making fun of her spirit drives and her attempts to help renovate the school. It seemed like Samantha had been standing in Kristine's way all through junior year.

Kristine headed for her locker, since she needed to pick up her workbook before language lab. On the way she passed two seniors who were walking close together. One was Michael Hume, a smart-mouthed clown. The other was Alma Martinez, someone Kristine rarely paid attention to. They were both friends of Samantha's.

The two seniors fanned out when they saw Kristine, forcing her to walk between them.

"Hey, Moore. Saw your play," Michael said, smirking.

Alma giggled. "I'm going next week. I've heard sooo much about it. Especially about your performance."

"Starlet Kristine," Michael cracked.

Kristine refused to look at them. They were members of Club, Club, Sam's pet organization. Club, Club was a holier-than-thou clique that wouldn't stoop to anything as déclassé as decorating for a football game or raising money to plant flowers in front of the cafeteria. No, they were too busy saving the whales, boycotting French cheese, or standing up for scuzzy lowlife kids who didn't even want to be in school.

Kristine kept walking, until she couldn't help but turn back. She glanced back just in time to see Alma and Michael falling over each other in silent guffaws. As soon as they saw Kristine, they pretended to be pointing at the world maps hanging outside Mr. Anderson's geography class. Stifling more laughter, they moved on.

Kristine felt humiliated. She strolled more quickly, imagining their conversation as she approached her locker.

"Her father bought her the part."

"Jen Dubrosky was the one who deserved it."

"Boy, did Jen get robbed."

"That Kristine is such a joke."

By the time Kristine focused on her locker, she felt like she was going to throw up again. Dizzy, she put her hands over her ears as if she could stop all the talk. Sure, *she'd* been spreading nasty gossip about Jennifer Dubrosky, but only because Jen had starting slamming her first. Besides, Jen had blabbed for herself. Jen had told another drama girl the whole gruesome tale. Of course, the story had gotten exaggerated. People were now saying that Jen had actually posed for porn films and that you could rent them at the local video store. Kristine knew that wasn't true, but she hadn't done anything to stop the buzz.

"What can I do?" she told herself. "Talk is just talk. Gossip is just . . . "

But then she reached for her locker door and realized that talk had turned into action. Her locker door was open. There hadn't been a locker check lately, and Kristine always made sure to close her locker ultra tight. Her combination hadn't been cracked. No. The whole lock was broken!

"What?" Kristine managed.

Her locker door had been pried open with some kind of tool. Kristine flung the door all the way open and checked the inside. Unlike most people, she didn't plaster pictures or bumper stickers on the inside of the door. She liked her locker super neat, and only used it to stow books and school supplies. But her books had been knocked over and the pile was a lot smaller than it had been the day before. It took her about five seconds to see what was missing.

"My new books!" Kristine gasped. Almost a hundred dollars worth. They were the new hardbacks that Dawn had picked up for her at Garo's. The research volumes for her fairness speech. Kristine still needed those books. So far, she'd only written the outline.

Kristine looked up and down the hall, not sure

what to do. Her head was light now and tears pressed at the back of her throat. Of course, she would report the theft. She could even buy new copies of the books. If Garo was out, her father would call around until he located copies elsewhere. It wasn't just the loss of the books that was getting to her. It was the invasiveness of the theft, the meanness, the obvious desire to hurt her and pull her down.

What was going on!

Kristine began crying just as the first bell went off. She'd never cried in school before, and she didn't want anyone to see her or hear her uncontrolled little gasps. People like Jennifer Dubrosky got weepy on campus and locked themselves in the girls' can.

Not Kristine Moore.

Kristine took deep breaths and tried to swallow back her tears. She had eight minutes until the tardy bell. She faced her locker, hiding from the kids that were suddenly pouring in at an alarming rate. There was a girls' bathroom nearby, but Kristine knew that it would be a crowded chaos of lipstick, chatter and smoke.

"The dressing room," Kristine remembered. "The theater dressing room."

If she could get to the theater dressing room undetected, she could finish her cry, fix her makeup and wash her face. She could collect herself for a few minutes, then emerge without a trace of humiliation or pain. And she wouldn't run into anyone, since the theater held no first-period class.

Kristine moved quickly, not meeting anyone's eye until she got away from the crowd and slipped in the theater's back entrance. Feeling safe at last, she let out a sob. She hurried along the concrete corridor, then threw open the dressing room door.

"Uhhh."

Kristine froze. She'd made a mistake, she told herself. She was in the middle of a nightmare. Shattered glass covered the floor. Her mirror was graffitoed. Her makeup and flowers had been thrown on the floor. She'd walked into the wrong room . . . the wrong school . . . the wrong planet, she told herself. She had to turn around and start over.

But then she looked again.

The words were both terrifying and humiliating. They seemed to pulse at her with a life of their own.

DADDY'S GIRL . . .

SICK . . .

PHONY . . .

Kristine couldn't look anymore. She slammed the door shut and threw herself against the concrete dressing room wall.

"WHO DID THIS TO ME?" she wept as she pounded the wall. "WHY DID THEY DO THIS? WHO IS DOING THIS?"

She hit with her fists. She kicked with her cowboy boots until her toes stung. Then she just fell onto the cold hard floor, cutting her hand on a shard of glass from the broken flower vase.

The tardy bell rang, but Kristine ignored it.

She had such a spotless record that she could afford a tardy for once. She stayed huddled on the floor until she was finally able to stop crying. She licked the blood from the cut on her hand.

She looked around at the broken glass, the scattered flowers and the graffiti. She felt so lonely and angry that she wanted to rip down the roof.

Slowly, she stood up. She picked up one dried out rose and pricked her finger on a thorn. For a moment she wasn't sure what else to do. Then she realized that the most important thing was for no one else to see what had been done to her.

For the time being, no one must know.

So very slowly, very carefully, Kristine began to clean up. Taking in each word of graffiti, each splinter of glass and dried-out flower, she picked up the pieces. She cleaned the mirror, using an entire box of tissues. She stowed the dirty Kleenex in her purse, lest someone put together the leftover clues. She picked up the wrecked pieces of makeup and hid them away, too.

Finally Kristine sat at her dressing space and looked at her sad face in the mirror.

She dried her eyes.

She would still report the theft of her books, Kristine decided.

But she would keep this humiliation to herself . . . at least until she got through that night's performance. After that, she would figure out exactly what she was going to do.

The scrape on Camille's face was starting to heal. Her cheek still felt stiff and her bruises had turned smoggy sunset shades of lavender and yellow. She'd started painting glittery pink around the edges of her wound, then matching it with dabs of golden glitter around her eyes.

"What did the doctor say this morning?" Sam asked as they walked across the West L.A. High quad. It must have been ninety degrees, even though it was only midmorning break.

Camille was already feeling sweaty in a short skirt, boxy jacket, long purple scarf and running shoes. "Nothing."

Kristine Moore's spirit groupies were unrolling butcher paper and stood with paint and brushes ready. Sam delicately stepped over the paper and ignored Dawn Warrington's dirty looks. "Camille."

Camille stopped to read the spirit poster, which cheered on the track team for that weekend's meet. She also noticed the scowls and whispers from the Kristinettes, but she didn't want to think about silly Dawn or snotty Stacy DeFonte. She had too many other things battling inside her head.

Picking up her pace, Camille quickly left the quad and entered the cool shade of the main hall. The spirit monsters were in there, too. They were painting a bank of lockers with blue enamel.

"Girlfriend," Camille answered Sam. She tried to maintain her usual sassy confidence. "I'm fine. I'm better than fine. The doctor doesn't even think I'll have a scar." She laughed. "I was beginning to worry that when I got my own talk show, they'd only be able to photograph me from one side."

Sam twirled around and walked backward to block Camille. In baggy overalls and backward baseball cap, she reminded Camille of a dead-end kid. "Camille, you were in the hospital! You were hit by a car! Nobody knows who hit you! I'm sure the doctor is worried about more than whether or not you'll have a scar."

Camille hugged her heavy stack of books. She hadn't even wanted to go back to the doctor that morning. Her mother had had to force her out the door, like some wacked-out five-year-old on her first day of kindergarten. At the doctor's office, Camille had barely listened to the questions. She'd just recited, *Fine. No problems. No blurry vision. No nausea. No, no. No headaches. No concerns.* She'd almost told the truth.

"I'm fine!" she barked again.

Sam raised her arms and backed up. "Okay, okay."

Camille slowed down and led the way past the library, where she spotted Barry Barsumian just leaving the reference desk. She tried to remember what Barry's speech topic was, then told herself that she'd probably never known his topic in the first place.

Phew.

Camille would never admit what was really bothering her. She hadn't even mentioned it to the doctor. She was having trouble remembering things. It wasn't like some old movie where she didn't recognize Sam, or couldn't remember what she'd done during sophomore year. It was just the occasional name or noun that escaped her. The previous night she'd been telling her mom about the track meet coming up. Suddenly she hadn't been able to remember the word "hurdle." It wasn't a word she used a lot, and there was no reason that it should have been on the tip of her tongue. It was just that Camille had never forgotten words before.

Another thing that bothered Camille was the feeling she got when she walked in front of a car. Her heart would speed up. Her breathing would get shallow. She found herself avoiding crosswalks and corners. She'd developed an insane route onto campus, circling around the gym, through the zeroscrape project and then through the cafeteria kitchen—all to avoid crossing the teachers' parking lot.

Most troubling of all was that Camille still couldn't remember the accident. She'd start to have flashes of motion and light, but that was as far as it went. She sensed that the information was somewhere inside her head. She was beginning to think that she'd even seen the driver and the car. But she couldn't unlock the memory.

"Sam, did your mom or Carlos find out anything more?" she hinted, trying to act as if she didn't care. "Have they found any witnesses?"

"I don't think so." Sam stopped at the farthest library window and pointed to a poster that advertised the headline, "She Talks To Teens. And She Listens, Too." Underneath was a picture of Alison, in full LAPD blues.

Sam shuddered. "You know, my mom is coming to school today."

"Oh right. We have that assembly during fifth period." Camille worried. "Darn. I wanted to work on my journalism article. Think your mom will forgive me if I get out of it?"

Sam didn't answer for a moment. "I wish I could get out of it," she finally mumbled. "My mom barely told me about this. She's been working on this new project for juvenile crime intervention. All of sudden she tells me that she's going to show up at this school."

Camille finally focused on Sam. Sam looked surprisingly tired. Usually her freckled face looked sunny and pink. Now she had gray circles under her eyes. Her skin looked dull. Even

Kenny had mentioned that Sam had been acting flaky, as if she were hiding something. "Is this a big deal? Are you really upset about this?"

Sam shrugged. "I don't know. It guess it reminds me of those DARE assemblies we had in fifth grade. Never mind. I think I'm worried about Jen."

Camille didn't say anything. She'd heard the new rumors, too. Everyone had guesses about who had really hit Camille. And now someone had stolen books out of Kristine Moore's locker. Kristine was dropping hints about Jen being the thief. People were saying that the school wasn't safe anymore. Of course, West L.A. High had never been safe. But now Kristine's crowd clutched their Coach bags too tightly. They looked fifteen times before crossing the street.

Camille also sensed that there was more to it. Sam was holding back. "Are you sure that's all that's bugging you?" Camille asked. "Is there anything else going on? You and Jen have both been acting kind of spacey this week."

"Me and Jen?" Sam reacted. "What do you mean? Did Jen tell you something?"

Now Camille was starting to feel left out. Did Jen have some terrible secret that she would share only with Sam? Camille couldn't imagine it, but sometimes people surprised you. "No. Should she have told me something?"

Sam was about to say something, then changed her mind. "No. It's nothing. Never mind."

Camille had the distinct impression that it wasn't nothing. "What about Kenny and Dylan?"

"Nothing new." Sam sighed.

"Really?"

"Same, same."

"So, it's a lot of nothing new, same, same?"

Sam shrugged and Camille wondered why she was quizzing her. People had a right to be moody. Sam had a right to keep a secret or just not feel like spilling her guts. Just like Camille had a right not to remember somebody's name. It all didn't have to mean something!

Not feeling any better, Camille said good-bye to Sam and hurried past the library. Instead of going to her third-period class, she was due in the teachers' conference room. There, along with the other five finalists for the Governor's Award, she was having an orientation about the rest of the Award competition. Taking a deep breath, she rounded the corner and almost ran smack into Rafe Danielson.

"Hi, Rafe," she said, feeling almost shy. She looked down and noticed a milk spot on her skirt.

"Hey, Camille."

Camille blushed. Guys didn't turn her head very often, but Rafe was so handsome, with that surfer hair that fell over one eye, the golden tan and warm, carefree smile. He wore a hooded West L.A. sweatshirt and high tops that made his feet look really big. He took big, jockish strides as if he were on roller blades. Camille considered asking him how things were going with Jen, but just then Kristine appeared, too, wearing some casual-looking denim number that must have cost more than a month in the Yale dorms.

Camille decided that the best plan was just to go into the conference room.

"In we go," she sighed.

Once inside, everybody seemed edgy. Nerdy Barry had his nose buried in his research book. Suria sat sleek and regal, her dark hair pulled straight back so that she looked like an Egyptian princess. Dylan and Rafe indulged in a little jockish joking, but even that didn't last long, especially when Kristine sat down right between them, nervously twiddling her diamond stud earrings.

They were settled around a long table that had been decorated with what looked like a sculpture class centerpiece. In front of each chair was a folder, filled with printouts and forms. The formality of it was intimidating. Soon there wasn't a sound, except for quick breathing and the turning of pages.

Ms. Sanford, the counselor who was running the competition, breezed in after the tardy bell. Super-tidy and organized, she wore a fuchsia tee shirt dress, Birkenstock sandals and earrings that looked like bunches of fruit. She was famous for being the only faculty member who wore braces.

Ms. Sandford began immediately. "How is everyone today?" She didn't wait for an answer. "I'll go over all of this quickly." She grinned, showing off her orthodonture, which featured pink wires. "I know you're all good students and you'd like to get back to class."

Rafe and Suria made faces, implying that their third periods were nothing to write home about.

"Anyway," Ms. Sanford went on, "I wanted to make sure that you all knew what the upcoming schedule was. We're getting to the nitty-gritty of the contest, and I want you all to do your best."

Suria smiled.

Dylan rubbed his eyes.

Ms. Sanford pulled out a pink paper and instructed the students to do the same. "You can see that the speeches are scheduled for Monday night, in The Little Theater. You'll each have eight minutes. Any questions?"

No one raised a hand. They'd all known about the speech format for some time.

Ms. Sanford barely stopped for breath. "The deadline for your teacher recommendations is tomorrow. I think most of your letters have come in. I mainly wanted to let you know about the final ceremony, where we will announce the winner."

Everyone sat up.

Ms. Sanford grinned. "Of course, you're all winners, and just to have made it to the finals is a tremendous accomplishment. But there will be one winner chosen, and that person's name will be announced on Saturday night at an award dinner and ceremony in the cafeteria."

Again, Dylan and Rafe exchanged looks. They would both have a track meet that same weekend. Suria would have a swim meet, too. She let out a little moan.

Noticing Suria, Dylan and Rafe, Ms. Sanford

added, "Don't waste time trying to figure out who is gathering the most points. We won't complete the tally until right before the ceremony." She winked at the boys. "So, even the last athletic meets will count."

Barry tapped his pen on the tabletop.

Ms. Sandford dug in a manila envelope and pulled out a stack of baby blue tickets. "Each of you gets four free passes to the dinner." She smiled at Kristine. "The Social Activities Committee is providing the food. We know that our old cafeteria isn't the most glamorous place in town, but the committee will do its best to spiff things up."

Kristine gloated. "You're welcome," she mouthed.

Ms. Sanford slid off the rubber band and passed the tickets around. "And you can buy more tickets in the attendance office. If anyone needs more freebies for immediate family, just come talk to me. The Social Committee has something yummy planned."

"As if any of us are going to feel like eating," Suria cracked. She wrapped her arms around her muscular body and huffed.

Ms. Sanford laughed. "It will be very exciting. Now, I'll let you all hurry on to your classes. You'll have that police assembly during three different periods today. I don't want to take any more of your class time."

Everyone stood up, then realized that Ms. Sandford had one last thing to say.

"Remember," she announced. "We will be

looking into your backgrounds, your behavior and your records. If there are any secrets in your past, you might as well tell me now. You won't be able to hide. You'll just be embarrassed by being disqualified later on."

Ms. Sanford looked around the table, gazing up at each pair of eyes. Each finalist matched her stare with confidence. Barry cleared his throat and Suria stood even taller.

"Good," Ms. Sandford pronounced. She stood up, too, and tapped her folder on the table. "I look forward to seeing you all at the speeches. And may the best student win."

All six of them hurried out, plowing into each other in the doorway. Barry stepped right on Camille's foot and didn't say excuse me. As Camille glared into his absent-minded professor eyes, she suddenly remembered the topic for his speech.

Technology and the Future.

Of course. Barry had told her a couple of weeks ago, when she'd run into him at L.A. Computerworks.

Taking a deep breath, Camille shouldered her way past Barry and Kristine and began to stride down the hall. It was all coming back, she realized. Scabby face or not, she was still five-hundred-watt Camille. Maybe some mysterious phantom had hit her with a car, but nobody had stolen her books. And if they had, they couldn't steal her smarts. She could still walk faster, talk faster and think faster than any other junior at West L.A. High.

"I am the best student," she said out loud. "And I am going to win."

Loser, loser, loser.

What a horrible word.

Look it up in the dictionary.

One who doesn't win . . . doesn't get the prize, the chance, the glory. Watching someone else grab the spotlight when I should have been the one.

It should have been me.

It should have been me.

It should have been me.

"Narc."

"Pig."

"Narc-ette."

As Sam filed into the gym for the fifth-period assembly, she wished that she could temporarily go deaf. She wished that Kristine's father could operate on her face until no one would recognize her. She considered changing her name, dying her hair or walking around in a Halloween mask. Anything would be better than overhearing the names being used to describe her own mother.

"Heat."

"Narc."

"Oink, oink, oink."

Not that everyone knew that Alison was Sam's mom. Sam had never advertised the fact that her mother was a cop. Actually, her mom hadn't been on the force for very long. And when her mom had worked for the police department as a dispatcher, Sam had just said, "Oh, my mom works in an office."

That had been true, Sam told herself, as she joined the herd of juniors that were bottlenecked in the gym's double doors. Precinct house was sort of another name for office, even though Sam didn't know of any other office that had its own jail. She stopped to take off her lace-up boots, then got shoved against the foyer wall.

"Settle down, settle down!" barked Boys' Vice Principal Sizar, who was inside the gym screaming into a bullhorn. "Sit down on the floor and let's get started!"

Sam hugged her boots and padded in, feeling the cold floor through the hole in her sock. While she searched for her friends, six-foot-five, ex-pro football player Sizar whistled so loudly that everyone groaned. He snapped his fingers at a few rowdy kids, who were piling on top of each other. Sam spotted her mother waiting behind Sizar. Sam wished that, just this once, Sizar would lighten up his act.

Sam finally found Kenny, who took off his bowler hat and waved it at her. She stepped over and around some friends from English class, then huddled down between Kenny and Jen. Kenny tickled her ankle as she sat, but Jen barely looked up. With each passing day, Jen seemed to look more and more haunted. She was wearing the same lavender jumper she'd worn the day before. Her beautiful hair was tangled and fell over her face. Sam remembered the little airplane vodka bottle and prayed that Jen wasn't drinking anymore.

"Hi," Sam whispered as she sat.

Kenny tapped her with his algebra book.

Jen just sighed.

Huddling close to Jen, Sam tried to tell if there was liquor on her breath. Then she remembered that vodka didn't smell, and that she didn't know what booze smelled like anyway. So Sam checked out the two hundred plus students gathered in the gym. As promised, Camille had stayed in the journalism room. Sam couldn't even find Dylan, then remembered that only a third of the class was due for assembly during this period.

"QUIET!" Sizar belted.

Sam saw her mother cringe. Alison must have known that Sam was in the crowd, but she didn't look for her. Sam didn't try and attract her mom's attention either. Instead, she watched Kristine Moore, who was kneeling a few feet away, on top of someone else's jacket. Sam hadn't seen much of Kristine since she and Jen had trashed the theater dressing room.

Sam and Jen hadn't mentioned what they'd done since that night. Once Sam had tried to discuss it with Jen, but Jen had started to cry. To Sam's incredible relief, no one else had mentioned it either. Sam didn't know if Kristine had even found the mess, or if the janitor had come across it first and cleaned the whole thing up. That seemed unlikely. Someone had to know about it. The whole incident haunted her, too.

Sam was ashamed of what she'd done. And she had the feeling that Jen felt the same way.

Vice Principal Sizar held up his big, hairy arms. "As soon as it's absolutely quiet, I'll introduce our special guest." He then proceeded to take a safety pin out of his pocket and raise it over his head. Everyone groaned. He always did this stupid routine of waiting until he could hear a pin drop. The whole student body hated it. Sure enough, he dropped the pin. He had to drop it three times before he was satisfied.

Jen cringed.

Sizar gestured for Alison to step forward. She was wearing LAPD blues again. Sam didn't know why her mom had shown up in uniform. When Alison had been hired to handle juvenile problems, she'd insisted that uniforms were intimidating. She usually worked in plainclothes.

"I'm very pleased to introduce Officer Alison Crane of the Los Angeles Police Department," Sizar continued. "Officer Crane has a particular interest in working with young people. She's devising a new program and she wants to tell you about it."

Alison thanked him. She adjusted her wire-rimmed glasses and smiled at the crowd. Her uniform made her look bulky and masculine, as if she were wearing somebody else's clothes.

"Did you know about this assembly?" Jen whispered to Sam in an uptight voice. She chewed on a fingernail. "Your mom looks so official. Is that really a gun?"

Sam leaned toward her. "I knew Mom wanted to set up some kind of peer review thing, and she just got permission from her sergeant and the principal."

"QUIET!" the vice principal screamed.

Sam froze.

Jen buried her face in her hands.

"Shhhh." Kenny giggled.

Alison rested her hands on her hips, which made Sam stare at that black leather holster, too. The crowd was restless. People were nudging each other with stockinged feet, pinching bottoms and passing notes.

To Sam's surprise, Alison didn't move. She didn't yell like Vice Principal Sizar, or pull drop-the-pin tricks or threaten or beg. She just stood quietly, looking at all of them.

Eventually they quieted down. Then Alison started stepping over people, heading into the middle of the crowd. When she passed Sam, she touched Sam's shoulder, proving that she had seen Sam after all. Jen scooted back, as if she feared that Alison might touch her, too. Alison clambered over more bodies and books.

"Can you all just get in a big circle?" Alison asked in a relaxed voice. "This doesn't need to be so formal."

People shifted, tempted to laugh at Alison, but also starting to get curious. Sizar offered a chair, but Alison wouldn't take it. That was when Sam noticed that her mom had taken off her shoes.

Alison wandered into the center of the circle

in her LAPD blues, black holster, permed straw-colored hair and bare feet. On the way she took off her uniform cap and exchanged it for Kenny's black bowler. Kenny mugged in her police cap and everyone laughed.

"Sorry about this uniform," Alison began. "My boss insisted. It was sort of like when you have to dress up for Sunday dinner at your grandparents'. You know you don't really look like yourself, but you also know that it's not worth fighting over."

Everyone laughed. Then they sat back and watched Alison. The nudging and notes-passing had stopped.

"I guess, that's what this assembly is about," Alison explained in a friendly voice. She took off Kenny's hat and flipped it back to him like a Frisbee.

He caught it with one hand.

"This is about trying to solve problems using common sense. It's about trying to do away with some of the rules that are just empty rules. Instead, I'd like to think about helping people to take responsibility for their actions, and to be productive members of their community."

The gym had become totally quiet.

"I'm on the streets almost every day," Alison continued. "I talk to teens. Sometimes I give them rides or buy them lunch. Sometimes I hassle them. Sometimes I arrest them." She put a hand over her brow and squinted. "I think I even recognize a few of you," she teased.

Ron Claussen, a notoriously wild junior, let

out a bellowy laugh. He was the definition of *attitude.*

Alison winked at him. "Okay, Ron. Let's take you for example. Can I do that? Can I tell your classmates what I know about you?"

Ron was a wiry wrestler who'd been rumored to be in a gang. He strutted up, then put his arm around her and grinned. Alison didn't seem to mind.

"I got no secrets," he bragged.

"Okay." Alison looked out at the crowd. "A few weeks ago, Ron was kind of loaded. Is that accurate, Ron?"

Ron grinned.

Alison pressed on. "Ron was horsing around down on Sierra Madre Avenue, and he grabbed his girlfriend's high heel away from her. When Ron's friend tried to get her shoe back, Ron threw it—right through the living room window of a house belonging to a woman named Rosa Cruz."

"It was an accident, man," Ron laughed.

"I believe that you didn't mean to break that window, Ron," Alison agreed. "But look at Rosa's side of it. Rosa's two small children were in the living room when that window shattered. They were terrified. They could have been seriously hurt. Rosa said it sounded like a bomb exploded in her house. Her youngest daughter still cries about it and has trouble falling asleep. Nobody was there to help comfort Rosa's kids. Nobody helped Rosa clean up the broken glass. And Rosa doesn't have insurance, so she had to pay two hundred and forty dollars out of her own pocket to get her window fixed."

Ron looked sheepish.

Sam thought about the trashed dressing room and wanted to crawl inside her turtleneck. Jen had begun to tremble and chew her fingers.

"What do you think would be fair and responsible here?" Alison asked.

Everyone looked serious.

"I could arrest Ron," Alison suggested, "which will give him a record that will stick with him until he's eighteen. That could prevent him from getting a job, or doing other things that might really make his life more interesting."

Kids whispered to each other.

"I could drag Ron to the station and try and scare him," Alison said. "I could even send Ron to juvenile detention and juvenile court. I suspect that Ron will get in a heap of trouble at home, but I'm not sure that any of that will really change Ron's behavior. In fact, it might make things even harder for Ron. And it sure doesn't help Mrs. Cruz. So what do you think I should do?"

Hands shot up.

Alison began pointing.

"You should have made Ron clean up the glass."

"Ron should do something to help Mrs. Cruz."

"Ron should pay to fix her window!"

People cheered.

Ron shuffled back to his place.

"But Ron doesn't have two hundred and forty dollars, do you, Ron?" Alison pointed out.

Ron was starting to sulk. "No way."

"So what's fair now?" Alison pressed. "And what will make Ron think twice before he gets so loaded that he accidentally throws a shoe through someone's window again?"

Sam glanced around. The juniors were really getting into this. Some people were consulting one another. Others were deep in thought. Kenny had put away his homework and was sitting up very straight. Jen, however, still sat with her hands over her face. Sam touched Jen's back, but Jen flinched away from her.

Robert Owens, a New Age-type in tie-dye and sandals, shot to his feet. "Like Ron could work so many hours doing stuff for Mrs. Cruz, until she feels like he's really paid her back. Like for everything, you know."

"And maybe he could do something else for the community, too," Kenny added, "like clean the park, or paint over graffiti there."

When Kenny mentioned the word graffiti, Sam's stomach clenched.

Jen let out a tiny groan.

Alison grinned. "Thanks, Kenny. That's a great idea. Because we are all a community here, aren't we?"

Everyone nodded.

"You know, you're all way ahead of me," Alison told them. "It took me all month to think this up, and you all figured it out in the last ten minutes."

"We did?" Someone giggled.

"What did we figure out?"

"We're so smart."

Alison raised her hands and immediately got the attention of the crowd again. "I'll tell you what you figured out."

Sam couldn't believe it. Her mom had gone from being a "narc," to the hippest, warm and fuzzy mom cop in L.A. She had the junior class wrapped around her finger.

"And I thought it was *my* plan," Alison joked. She crouched down and everyone moved in. "Since you all have such good ideas and good judgment, I'm going to start a Peer Review Board at West L.A. High."

"Huh?"

"What's that?"

"Peer review?"

Alison gestured for quiet again. "When a student breaks a school rule or a law, they will appear before a jury of their peers, and those fellow students will be the ones to dole out a punishment. This system will only apply to first offenders—so if you have a record, or if you've already been in trouble, then you deal with the police. And this will only apply to misdemeanor or minor crimes. We're going to start with problems that occur on campus. If that seems to work, we'll expand into off-campus problems, too."

While the students stopped to chatter, Alison gestured to Vice Principal Sizar. He stepped over a few kids and handed her a clipboard. Alison looked over the papers attached, then held up the board. "I have a list of the first set of crimes that we are going to try. And I'm going to announce them. We are not keeping secrets here. This is a public forum, and in fact the peer trials will be public, too."

Sam wondered what crimes would be on her mom's rap sheet. The gossip mill had already convicted Caroline Shaw of drinking during that Friday night Destroyer dance. Sure enough, Caroline's was the first name to be announced. Devon Russell and Pete Thomas had gotten into a fistfight in the cafeteria. Betty Kai Lee had been caught with some pills during locker search.

Lastly, were two unsolved crimes. Someone had stolen books from Kristine Moore's locker—tsk, tsk. And the second crime involved school property, so Alison let Vice Principal Sizar address the crowd again.

The VP stood on the edge of the gym floor and barked, "Okay. This happened last night and I'm very angry about it." He glowered. "Somebody spray painted black paint on our stadium spirit sign. We all worked hard last fall to get that spirit logo professionally made. Our athletes deserve better!"

Sam knew what Sizar was referring to. There was a sign at the edge of the bleachers that announced the team name in high relief, Day-Glo letters. Someone had sprayed over it with black paint? Why would any West L.A. High student do that? Especially when the track team was doing so well?

Jen hugged herself and shivered.

"Our track team is putting their guts on the line right now," Sizar threatened. "And I won't tolerate this kind of insult."

"Maybe it wasn't somebody from our school," Heather Cruikshank suggested.

Heads nodded. Most people seemed to agree that the damage *must* have been done by someone from a rival student body. But Sizar didn't seem convinced. Jen just kept fidgeting and shaking. Sam wasn't sure what to think.

"Is there anything else that anyone would like to bring up?" Alison asked, taking charge again.

Everyone was still discussing the spirit sign. Sam breathed a sigh of relief. She didn't dare look at Jen again, or mention the dressing room incident.

"I wanted to present these assemblies in smallish groups, so that you could bring up any concerns," Alison said. "I'll be on campus frequently just to talk, to check in, to help in any way that I can. Is there anything else?"

There were a few moments of quiet. Everyone was reaching for books and sweaters when, suddenly, someone rose from the gym floor. Unlike all the other students who had been waving their hands and jumping up, this girl rose like graceful smoke. She slowly wove her way around, heading for the middle of the circle. She wore a tight knit gray dress and a delicate red scarf. Her blond hair was twisted in a French braid and her tights skidded noiselessly along the shiny, gym floor.

It was Kristine Moore.

Sam shivered.

Jen froze.

When Kristine finally reached Alison, she said, "Last Thursday night, or maybe it was early Friday morning, someone broke into the school theater dressing room. They found my dressing space, where I get ready for the school play. They broke my vase of roses, which my father had given me. They wrecked some of my makeup." Her voice caught. "And they wrote horrible things all over my mirror."

Alison listened with concern.

Sam barely breathed.

The other juniors were quiet. They had never seen Kristine so hurt before.

"I guess you could call this crime vandalism, or defacing school property," Kristine stated, trying to keep her emotions under control. Oddly, she sounded much more poised and compelling than she had on stage. "And destruction of my property, too." Her mouth started to quiver. "They wrote such mean things," she blurted. "Terrible things."

Kristine's groupies looked outraged.

"It sounds like someone was very cruel to you," Alison soothed. "Not that we can't pursue this crime—and I agree that it is a crime. But it also sounds like someone really wanted to hurt you. And I think they succeeded."

"Yes," Kristine gasped. She stopped for a moment, unable to speak. Everyone had been talking about how bad she'd been in the play.

They'd been wondering if her father was going to show up at all four performances. Now Sam could feel the wave of sympathy rolling back in Kristine's favor.

"Do you have any idea who did it?" Alison asked.

"All I know is that whoever did it left this behind." Kristine pulled a clenched hand out of her pocket and presented a tiny envelope, like the kind used to store rare coins or small pieces of jewelry. She handed the envelope to Alison.

Alison checked her watch. The class period was almost over. She stuck the envelope in her pocket.

"Anyway," Kristine sniffed. "I found that in the dressing room when I cleaned everything up. I know that it doesn't belong to anyone in *The Rainmaker*, because I asked. And I know it wasn't there before, because I found it in my personal makeup box. So I think it belongs to the person who wrecked my dressing space."

Alison was about to speak again, when Kristine burst into tears. This was no act, Sam had to admit. Kristine had already proved that she had no acting talent.

Alison took Kristine in her arms and hugged her until the bell rang. Then Kristine wobbled back to her admirers, who had gathered her purse and her books.

Jen was having trouble standing up. She was still wobbly when Kenny accidentally bumped into her. Suddenly Sam noticed that Kristine was glaring . . . at her and at Jen.

Luckily Alison was distracted, reminding everyone to check the Peer Review board near the library and sign up for jury duty. Kenny, who had gym next period, hurried off toward the boys' shower room.

"Why is Kristine looking at us?" Jen whispered. "Do you think she knows?"

"She was looking at *me*," Sam decided. She suddenly remembered the book theft and wondered if Jen could have been responsible for that. No. It wasn't possible.

Jen grabbed Sam and whispered, "I'll die if she finds out. She'll make my life horrible. She already has. She can't know it was me. Ever."

Sam didn't know what to do. The crowd was shifting towards the door, where the next group of students was waiting to come in. Sam sensed that Jen wasn't going to move until Sam promised to protect her. "Don't worry," she whispered. "The only person who knows is me, and I won't rat on you, Jen. I won't tell."

Jen had turned white. She clutched Sam's arm so hard that she was leaving marks. "I don't know what to do, Sam. I don't know what to do."

Sam didn't know what to do either. All she knew was that she and Jen had gotten themselves into a very big mess.

10

Sam climbed up the fire escape that led to her second-story apartment roof. Her recycling bag was full of books and the strap cut into her shoulder. Still she climbed, rung after rung after rung. The metal was hot from the late afternoon sun, but it was an easy climb onto the expanse of tar paper that she and her mom rented along with their apartment.

Once on the roof, Sam felt a little better. It was hot up there, too, but the warmth was comforting. Since that assembly at school, she'd felt like someone was following her. She'd shivered through her last two classes, jumped at every little sound. At the same time, she'd barely heard anything. When the principal had peeked her head into Sam's English class, Sam had almost leapt up and screamed, *Okay, I did it!,* but the principal had just been saying Hi, and then had disappeared again with nothing more than a watchful eye.

What was the principal watching for?

Drinking?

Stealing?

Vandalizing another spirit sign?

What about hit-and-run accidents?

What was really going on at school!

Sam crouched down on the edge of her roof and looked out at the smoggy sky, which was crisscrossed with wires and hook-ups for cable TV. Then she shifted and glanced back over her own rooftop. She didn't want to think about school any more. The picnic table that she'd painted electric blue was strewn with leaves. Her potted flowers looked thirsty. Even her strung Christmas lights seemed to droop.

Even though Sam had neglected her rooftop patio of late, it was still her favorite place in L.A. Maybe it was just being high up that soothed her. On the roof she could feel both private and free. It was the first time that day that she hadn't felt overwhelmed with worry and guilt.

Even so, she would have to climb back down and go through the lobby if she wanted to get into her apartment. The only way to get from the roof into the living room was through an old double hung window that locked on the inside. Her mom had been working the late shift on Fridays, so the window would be secured. Sam picked up her book sack again and glanced down.

"Hello again, fire escape," she sighed. Even though it was only one story, getting up was always easier than lowering herself back down. "That's sure what I need. Escape."

Sam felt a surge of lightheadedness and waited to catch her breath. Everybody was crowding in on her. Jen seemed spaced-out and guilt-ridden, except when she went gaga talking about Rafe. Then again, Sam hadn't actually seen Jen and Rafe together. But she knew that Rafe was busy with track and the Governor's Award. And Jen seemed so preoccupied with . . . Sam wasn't sure what all was bothering Jen, and she wasn't sure she wanted to know. Of course Jen was still freaked over the porn incident, and the gossip that followed. Then there was the play and the dressing room horror. There seemed more than enough reason for Jen to be out of sorts, and yet Sam sensed that there might a whole lot else . . .

"Maybe Rafe will pull Jen out of this. I don't know."

Sam let her feet dangle over the roof edge. Then there was Camille, another escape artist if Sam ever saw one. Camille was in super-achiever mode, but was she also trying to escape the fact that she'd been seriously hurt? Why couldn't they find out who had hit Camille? Why had no one seen the accident? And why would anyone hit a pedestrian and then just speed away?

Lowering her feet onto a rung, Sam thought about the people she needed to escape from right now. Kristine, of course. Sam didn't need to escape from Dylan, because he was already escaping from *her*. But Kenny. Sometimes Sam felt like everything with Kenny was just right, and other times she wished she could escape back to when they had just been friends. She considered going down to his apartment. Then she remembered with relief that he'd stayed after school to rehearse with the jazz band.

And then there was her mother. Sam had missed her mom so much when her mom had been on shift every night, but now her mother was going to become a fixture at school. And that was another thing that made Sam want to escape.

In fact, just as Sam started to lower herself onto the fire ladder she heard the living room window slide open.

Her mother called, "Sam, is that you? I'm home early, Sam. SAMMY?"

"It's me," Sam called back. She crawled back up onto the roof.

"Come on in," Alison commanded.

Sam took one last breath of warm, smoggy air, then shuffled past the vents and flower boxes. She picked one cherry tomato, but it was hard and sour. Then she climbed through the living room window and dumped her books on the floor.

Her mom was sitting in their old flea market rocking chair. She was working on a small laptop computer that had just been given to her by the police department. Her uniform jacket hung on the coat tree in the hall. Now Alison wore leggings and a big, sloppy sweater.

"I'm almost done with this," Alison murmured. "How long have you been out on the roof?"

Sam heard a funny sound in her mom's voice. Her mom didn't sound angry, just serious. Very serious. Sam walked right past her. Their apartment was a small two-bedroom that they'd decorated with secondhand treasures combined with modern finds from Pier One and Ikea. Sam wove under the hall arch and past her mother's desk in the foyer. In the kitchen, she stared into the fridge, then the cabinets. Finally, she stuck a packet of popcorn in the microwave.

"I thought you'd be on shift," Sam called. She watched the popcorn bag puff up.

"With this school project, my hours have changed." Alison's voice still had that funny tone. She sure didn't sound like the warm, fuzzy mom cop she'd been that afternoon at school. "That's one reason I wanted to do this project, so I'd be home with you more."

Sam poured the popcorn into a bowl and padded back to the living room. When she plopped down on the couch, her mom was just closing up her document. "What are you working on?"

Alison carefully turned off the computer. "I was doing another witness report on Camille's accident . . . or rather another non-witness with non-information. We can't find anyone who saw anything." Alison stared hard at Sam, then took a deep breath. "It seems like whoever hit Camille dropped down from outer space and then flew back up there." She took off her glasses and rubbed her eyes.

Sam munched popcorn. She reached for the TV.

Alison stopped her. "We need to talk," Alison said. She sat up and folded her hands.

Now Sam heard anger in her mother's voice, but didn't want to acknowledge it. "Kids liked you at school today," she offered. "They think this peer review thing is a good idea."

"That's good." Alison seemed to have barely heard her. She placed the computer under the coffee table. Then she reached to the side table next to the rocker and picked up a small, beige envelope. Alison held the envelope up, then slapped it down on the coffee table.

For a moment Sam just stared at it. Why was her mom bothering with this dramatic gesture? Then a zing of adrenaline went through her. She remembered that she'd seen that envelope before. It had been in Kristine's hand during the assembly.

"Do you know who gave me that?" Alison made sure.

Sam nodded. She'd broken out in a sweat. The popcorn had turned rancid in her mouth. "I think so."

"Open it."

Sam could tell that the envelope had been previously opened. Her fingers were greasy, so she wiped them on her jeans. Then she picked up the envelope and peered into it. At first, she didn't see anything. The envelope was so little. There was a lump inside the size of a gumball. Sam glanced up at her mom.

Alison was glaring with tired, blue eyes.

Sam turned the envelope upside down and

dumped the contents. At first nothing came out. Then there was a tiny *plink* as a small, round bead fell onto the coffee table.

Sam gasped audibly. It was the bead that Jen had made for her in art class. Painted with angels and flowers, it was the jewel that Sam had worn as a single earring, until she'd mysteriously lost it one week before.

Alison hadn't moved. "Would you like to explain?"

Sam felt like she was under interrogation. This wasn't fair! How dare her mother use police tactics on her? "Explain what?"

"Explain how your earring was found in Kristine Moore's makeup case. And would you also like to explain again why you were late coming home from school after the play?"

Sam's brain went into immediate overload, as if all her circuits had fired at once. She didn't know what to do. "You're acting like you already know," she said snottily. "So why are you asking me?"

"I want to hear it in your words," Alison said. "I want to know if it's really true."

Sam's head was still filled with static. She felt dizzy. The popcorn smell sickened her. Before she was really able to sort out her thoughts, she blurted, "It wasn't fair."

"What wasn't fair?"

"Kristine never should have gotten that part. It should have been Jen. Kristine's father paid to fix up the theater and that's why they gave the part to her. And then she had these flowers and all this expensive makeup. It wasn't right!"

"So the right thing was for you to destroy her property and draw cruel, hurtful things?"

Sam just wanted the whole incident to disappear. She knew she'd done the wrong thing. But she'd gotten carried away. And she'd wanted to make Jen feel better. This was all about Jen, Jen, Jen. "You don't understand . . . "

"Did you do it, Sam?" Alison demanded. "Is that why you were late coming home last week? Did you wreck Kristine's dressing space and did you lie to me?"

"YES!" Sam suddenly yelled. She burst into tears. "It was wrong. I know that what I did was wrong, too, but I couldn't stand it. And it just sort of happened. We didn't go in there thinking we were going to do that—"

"We?" Alison interrupted. She moved closer and put her hand on Sam's knee. "What do you mean, *we*?"

Sam held her breath.

"Sam. Look at me! You just said we. Was someone else with you when this happened!"

"I didn't say we," Sam backtracked. "I made a mistake."

"Jen went to the play with you that night?" Alison remembered. "Did Jen do it, too?"

Sam felt like she couldn't breathe. She'd promised to protect Jen. And if Kristine found out that Jen was part of this, Kristine wouldn't stop until Jen was totally destroyed.

"No," Sam lied. "Jen didn't do it." Sam

started to improvise, "Jen was flirting with Rafe Danielson, her new boyfriend. I had to wait for them, and I walked by the dressing room, um, alone, and I saw the flowers and everything, and I just got so angry!" Sam stopped for breath. She couldn't think of any more lies.

Alison looked skeptical. "I'm not sure I believe you, but we'll let it stand at that." She pulled out the clipboard that she'd used at the assembly that afternoon. "Sam, you will appear at the first peer review trial."

Of course. Sam wanted to spit. Of course.

"I'm not going to protect you," Alison threatened. "You are not getting any special treatment. You broke the rules, and I'm not going to go easy on you. You are going to treated like any other student at West L.A. High."

Oh no, I'm not, Sam wanted to shout. *I'll be treated like* your *kid. And I'll be judged much more harshly, because I'm the one who's never supposed to screw up.*

"Screw your courage to the sticking place and you'll not fail."

Kristine Moore watched herself in her dressing room mirror as she repeated Shakespeare's famous line. She was warming up for her fourth and final—thank God—performance of *The Rainmaker.* Her last evening of agony and humiliation.

She was the first cast member to arrive. It wasn't even six o'clock, but Kristine always arrived first. She didn't like anyone to see her without her makeup on.

"When Duncan is asleep . . . "

She'd begun her warm-up with the Lady Macbeth monologue she'd done for a speech tournament sophomore year. But now she remembered that the monologue hadn't even been good enough to get her past the first round of Dramatic Interp. If she'd had any brains, she'd have figured it out then.

"How can someone so smart be such an idiot?" she asked, forgetting Lady Macbeth and taking in her own perfect image.

Then she rifled through her book bag and pulled out a notice for a cast party. She posted it above the mirrors. Famous for her parties, she figured that a great party might make up for her dreadful performance. Unfortunately Mr. Kremer, the play production teacher, insisted that cast parties include all the drama students. But Kristine figured that she had all the drama students to win over again, so maybe his rule wasn't such a bad idea.

Eager to make use of her time alone, Kristine took off her Nordstrom's dress and hung it carefully. Then she slipped on an old oversized work shirt. She rubbed cold cream over her face until every speck of street makeup was off. She opened her tackle box and electric rollers. Then she sat down to curl her hair.

"Yuck."

She looked geeky without any makeup, but at least her mirror was clean. The ruined eye pencils had been replaced. Kristine had talked her father *out* of sending any more flowers. She hadn't told him about the dressing room incident, but she had managed to keep him from attending the play again on closing night.

"Oh Daddy," she heaved.

She stared at herself as she rolled her hair. What had ever made her want to become an actress? Real actresses were probably all sluts or flakes—like Jen—she told herself. No wonder she wasn't any good at it. Maybe she should think about becoming a news anchor instead. Or a movie producer. Everybody knew that actresses were unstable. She was much too refined to get in front of people and pretend.

Of course, her father always said she could be anything she wanted to be. And if there was anything she even hinted at wanting, he made sure it landed on her plate. Even this Governor's Award. Her dad had personally called the all teachers who'd written recommendations. Kristine didn't know what he'd said to them. But she had to wonder if he'd offered free eye jobs or discount liposuction.

"Oh no," Kristine remembered as she pinned up the last curler. The Governor's Award. In the middle of everything else, she still had that award to worry about. She was supposed to pick up some notes from her social studies teacher. She'd dropped off a draft of her speech for Mr. Congdon that morning. He'd promised to look it over, note suggestions, then leave it in the envelope taped to his door.

Kristine hesitated for a moment. Congdon's door was close by, just on the other side of the music room. It was only a few minutes after six, a time when the school was usually empty. Did she dare sneak out in her work shirt, curlers and bare, white legs?

She checked the mirror again. She'd be mortified if anyone saw her. On the other hand, if she waited until after the play, she'd probably forget. So she padded along the cold concrete, then skipped out into the hall.

As expected, the hall was deserted. She spotted Mr. Congdon's door and went right to it. Sure enough, there was her speech, right where the teacher had said it would be. Kristine glanced over his notes as she slowly wandered back.

Whack

"OW!"

"Sorry."

"Watch it!"

"I didn't see you. I said, sorry."

It all happened so fast that Kristine could hardly catch her breath. All she could think was that someone else was stealing her property or sneaking up on her to do something underhanded and mean. One moment she'd been reading Mr. Congdon's notes, and the next a guitar had smacked her in the stomach and her speech papers had scattered all over the floor.

"My speech!" she cried. "You did that on purpose!"

The boy who'd run into her put down his guitar and scrambled to pick up the papers.

That's when she recognized him as Kenny Sando Wilson, weirdo, nonconformist and nonidentical twin to Samantha Crane.

"I really didn't see you," he explained as he reached his long arms across the floor tiles. He was wearing a sleeveless denim vest that he'd probably decorated himself, with a hooded sweatshirt and baggy cut-offs. If Kristine hadn't known better, she'd have assumed he belonged to a gang.

"It was an accident. Geez."

"Right."

To Kristine's amazement, Kenny handed back her papers. He started to walk away, then noticed that she was wearing a man's shirt, no pants, no makeup and a huge head full of hair curlers. He stared. Then he smirked.

Kristine wanted to slug him. She wanted to throw something in his face, or kick him in the shin. Instead, she started to cry.

"Kristine," Kenny panicked. He took a step back, almost as if he were afraid of her.

"Go away!" she ranted. The harder she tried to stop crying, the more violently she heaved and sobbed. "All of you, everyone. GO AWAY!"

He didn't move. "I didn't mean to bump into you," he repeated. "I'm sorry."

"GO AWAY!!!!!!"

He just stood there.

She hated this! This was the fourth time she'd broken into tears at school. First, when she'd discovered that her books had been stolen. Then, for no reason at all, in the middle of

Advanced German she'd just totally lost it. In front of everyone at the assembly, she broken down sniveling. And now, in front of Samantha Crane's right-hand man, Kenny Sando Wilson, she was acting like a total loser.

"Forget it!" she cried. "Leave me alone." She put her hands to her naked face and started back down the hall.

To her amazement, Kenny followed her. "What is going on with you?" he asked. He'd left his guitar behind and was running his hand through his light brown afro. "You're so upset."

"Duh," Kristine shot back. She'd just seen Kimberly Barry, the stage manager for The Rainmaker, slip down the theater's back stairs. Despite losing it at school, Kristine had kept it together in front of her fellow drama students. That was her last frontier of pride.

Kristine looked back at Kenny, caught between the concern in his brown eyes and Kimberly's intelligent, busy figure stalled at the other end of the hall. Just then Kimberly was joined by Jeremy Lawrence, one of her fellow cast members.

Kristine had no choice. She inched back towards Kenny. Turning her back to Kimberly and Jeremy, she considered slugging Kenny in the chest. Instead, she put her hand on his arm.

He froze.

Kimberly and Jeremy wouldn't leave. Kristine knew that her face looked disgusting and red. They couldn't see her! She leaned into

Kenny and hid her face in his shoulder. For one quick moment she relaxed.

Kenny touched the back of her hair. Then he pulled out a red bandanna.

She stared at it and stepped away. This was Kenny, she remembered. He was the enemy. And he was a Samantha Crane-following weirdo.

"It's clean," he said, referring to the bandanna.

She just stared at it.

"I have a feeling that you don't want people to see you cry," he whispered. His voice was amazingly sweet. "So take my bandanna. Wipe your face. You'll be okay."

Kristine couldn't believe that he was being nice to her. She hated him! She'd always gone out of her way to snub him. She also remembered him kissing Samantha after the dance. She'd assumed that Sam and Dylan had been an item, so she'd been surprised to realized that Sam and Kenny had something going, too.

And she also always thought that Kenny hated her. Just like Sam hated her, and Jen, Camille, and the rest of that self-righteous, eccentric little crowd.

Kristine finally looked into Kenny's warm, dark eyes. She took the bandanna, then remembered that she had no makeup on. She wondered just how bad she looked.

When she tried to return his bandanna, Kenny said, "Keep it. It looks like you might need it again soon."

For some reason, Kristine suddenly wanted

to keep it. With all the flowers and opening night luck presents that she'd received for the play, not one had meant anything to her.

She had this weird feeling that Kenny's bandanna was the only present that might really bring her something good.

That feeling was back. And it was worse this time.

It felt like something had been building up inside, like those grade-school science experiments where something gave off more and more gas until it blew its top.

That was it.

Pounding head.

Raw, burning stomach.

Thoughts that exploded, despite all efforts to keep them under control.

Guilt.

Memories, too.

Today it was memories of disappointment. Of being ignored and put down. Being eight-years-old and getting up in front of the whole elementary school to sing solo for the Christmas program. It's all perfect, until the last line. Hitting the high note too hard. No. Voice splinters.

Dad says nothing. Mom doesn't even show. Afterwards, taking a sister's doll, putting her in a shoe box and burying her in the backyard.

Under a foot of dirt . . .

No one would hear her sing there.

No one would hear her crack.

The set for *The Rainmaker* was gone. No more weathervane, fence or horse blanket. Now the stage of The New Little Theater was decorated with a single poster announcing the names of the six Governor's Award finalists and the topics of their speeches. A bouquet of flowers sat on the other side of the stage and a podium was smack in the center. The only theatrical details left were the spotlights that focused on the speakers.

Camille sat in the front row, along with the other finalists: the judges—a local lawyer, a city councilwoman and a producer of TV documentaries—plus Ms. Sanford. Behind them was a theater full of parents, teachers and friends. Camille's mom and dad were a few rows back, dressed as if they were going to church. Behind them sat Sam and Jen. Sam had dressed up, too, in a miniskirt and secondhand man's sport coat with a fresh flower in the lapel. But Jen was looking more grungy and faded with each passing day. Her blond hair looked limp. Her long skirt clashed with her crocheted maroon vest.

Camille told herself not to think about Jen. Yes, her friend was still acting weird. Yes, there were beginning to be rumors saying that *Jen* had wrecked Kristine's dressing room. Jen had stolen Kristine's books. Maybe Jen had even been the one to spray paint the spirit sign, people were starting to say. Someone had even dared to say that Jen had driven the car that hit Camille. Insane. Ridiculous.

"Absurd."

But Camille had to get her mind off Jen and concentrate on her speech. She would be the fifth finalist to step up to the podium. Barry Barsumian had started things off. That meant that he had set the standard, which was hard, considering that he was practically a human computer. On the other hand, Barry was definitely lacking in the charm department. Next came Kristine, who had looked gorgeous, but whose presentation had been shaky. In the end, Kristine had seemed relieved to just get it over with.

Dylan, in contrast, had shone. He was the first speaker to really seem excited about his topic. He'd managed a few jokes. His speech about the Space Program had been so interesting that he'd actually made Camille forget her own nerves. After Dylan came Rafe, but his "Business and the Environment" speech was lackluster. Of course, Camille had barely listened to Rafe, since he was up right before her.

"Next we have Camille Weeks," announced Ms. Sanford as Rafe walked off the stage and plopped back down into his seat. The spotlights turned off while the judges hurried to jot down their notes.

Camille felt that familiar buzz of confidence

as she clutched her three-by-five cards and slowly climbed to the podium. Once there, she set out her cards and thanked Ms. Sanford, who had brought her a glass of water. As Camille waited for a "go" from the judges, she touched her face once, then decided that her scrape, which was shrinking daily, was sign of character, a little setback to be overcome. And she had overcome her accident, she decided. She felt that old Camille I-can-do-anything confidence. She smiled at her mother. Then she caught Sam's eye and smiled again.

Camille was ready to go, but just as she was about to begin, one of the judges had to run out—probably to go to the bathroom. The other two judges winked at Camille while she waited, stacking and restacking her cards. Then the audience began to chatter and the noise started to thicken. Trying to block out the rumble, Camille studied her notes. But the harder she focused on her notes, the more the chatter clashed and clanged inside her head. It was that untuned orchestra feeling again, and this time it made her ears ring.

Camille closed her eyes and took a deep breath. Her topic was "Free Speech and the Media." She'd researched at the libraries and on the Internet. She'd interviewed a lawyer friend of her father's and a journalist for the *L.A. Times*. She'd gone over her speech for her father, her debate coach and the USC political science professor who lived on her block. Nothing should have stopped her from being the best.

"Okay, we're ready now, Camille," Ms. Sanford announced. "Sorry for the wait."

Camille looked up in time to catch City Councilwoman Black slip back into her front-row seat. Then the spotlights flashed on, making a sound like a metal door closing. Two beams of light hit Camille. The glare was so bright that it made her eyes water.

Camille meant to begin her speech, but she couldn't take her eyes off the lights. Her mouth went dry. She couldn't remember where her glass of water was. Her heart sped up.

The lights . . . the headlights . . . they were coming at her, they were coming fast, she'd better run, she'd better get out of the way. Her legs . . . why wouldn't they move?

WHY COULDN'T SHE MOVE?

Suddenly Camille couldn't breathe either. Her heart was pounding so hard that it felt like a drum inside her chest. She was hot. She was *so* hot. She unbuttoned the top of her suit jacket. Her whole body felt like it was being suffocated in tight wool.

And then there were those lights again. Her heart thudded faster. She saw the flowers at the edge of the stage and then all she could see were the flowers at her grandmother's funeral. She saw the face of her grandmother in her open coffin, but then it was her own face, and the headlights kept coming . . . kept coming.

Camille was afraid she was having a heart attack—like her grandmother. She saw the headlights again, but this time she saw the car . . . the car that had hit her! It was coming after her and her grandmother was driving it . . . no, someone else was driving . . . someone she knew . . . *she could see the headlights, so why couldn't she see . . .*

Sweat broke out all over Camille's body. Her stomach was rolling like waves. She was so dizzy. She clutched the sides of the podium, knowing that she might fall. Then Ms. Sanford was standing on one side of her, and her father was standing on the other.

"What is it?" her father asked in a panicked voice.

"My speech," Camille managed. "I have to give my speech."

"Are you sick, Camille?" asked Ms. Sanford. "Camille, what's wrong?"

Camille looked out at the audience again. The headlights were gone now. Instead it was just a theater full of people, staring at her as if she'd just thrown up or lost her mind. The blouse under her jacket was soaked. Sweat dripped down the scrape on her face. Her legs began to shake.

"I'm sorry," she said.

"Don't be," her father assured her. "You're not feeling well, honey. Come on down. You don't have to do this. It's okay."

Camille wanted to tell him that she was fine. She wanted to give her speech. She needed to give her speech! But instead she let her father fold her in his arms and escort her off the stage. Her mother was waiting in the aisle and she swooped over. A moment later, the three of them were out the lobby door, drifting into the cool, night air. Camille struggled to avoid walking through the parking lot. She refused to cross in front of her father's car. Finally he had to lift her up and force her into the back seat. She lay there with her head in her mother's lap, but she just started shaking again.

"What is going on?"

"I think this school is cursed."

"That was scary. I've never seen Camille Weeks freak out like that."

"I've never seen anybody freak out like that."

"I heard that Camille is out of the contest now."

"No. But they gave her a zero for the speech, and that's twenty percent of the total score."

"So she might as well be out."

"I just hope she's okay."

"It's good luck for the other candidates. Camille would have been hard to beat."

"Lucky Kristine and Suria."

"Poor Camille."

Sam stood in the middle of the chatty crowd after Suria had finished her speech on "Keeping our Competitive Edge." It was a good thing that Suria was so relentlessly competitive, otherwise, she would never have been able to follow Camille. Sam wouldn't have been able to do it.

Other people had gone on rating the

candidates, but all Sam could think about was Camille. She'd been tempted to run out after Camille. But Camille's parents had had things under control, and Sam hadn't wanted to make things even more confusing. Now she just wanted to drive over to Camille's house and find out what was going on.

And then there was Jen.

"Jen!" Sam called. She didn't see Jen anywhere.

Sam was driving Jen home. Again. And Jen had disappeared. Again. Sam suspected that Jen was off flirting with Rafe. Again. That was fine with Sam. She just wished that Jen would check in with her once in a while.

Sam wandered over to the refreshment table. The crowd was thinning quickly, but there were still some cookies left. Kristine's groupies were hovering around the cider cups, but they made a purposeful exit when Sam walked over.

"Bye-bye." Sam glared. She grabbed a cookie and bit hard.

People knew about Sam and the dressing room incident—it had been added to the peer review trials and posted on the board outside the library. But Kristine's groupies had known even before Sam's crime had been published. And they were going out of their way to be nasty. If Sam walked by them in the hall, they gave her drop-dead looks. They slammed locker doors. When Sam had run into Dawn Warrington in the cafeteria, Dawn had intentionally knocked into her, slopping spaghetti all over Sam's shirt.

The Kristinettes turned up their perky noses at Sam and headed for the door. Sam tried not to be wounded, but she was already feeling unstable. Between Camille and Jen, she was starting to feel like she didn't have any friends left. Her whole world was going nuts.

Hoping to avoid any more of Kristine's fans, Sam backed away from the table. She stumbled over something, then reached out to keep from falling. She'd stumbled over a shiny loafer, one that was on Dylan's foot, attached to Dylan's leg. Now she was staring into Dylan's handsome face.

"Hello," she said.

Caught off guard, he actually looked her in the eye.

Don't walk away, she wanted to shout. *Don't you snub me, too!*

To her amazement, he didn't turn away. Maybe he was feeling so good about his speech that he didn't mind talking to her. He was wearing a sport coat that didn't quite fit, along with dress pants and those shiny loafers. He'd already stuffed his tie in his pocket and it looked like he'd just gotten a haircut. He had those flushed freckled cheeks that he'd get after his races and his green eyes looked confident and clear.

"Your speech was great," Sam managed. It was true. She didn't know what the judges had thought, but in her opinion, Dylan had outshone everyone.

"Thanks." He leaned over and took a cup of cider. "Is Camille okay?"

"I don't think so."

Dylan turned away. He was talking to her, but he wasn't exactly letting her in. Sam wondered if he'd heard about the dressing room incident, too. Maybe he thought she was some horrible delinquent. She was ready to ask him about it, but then he turned back and brought the subject up first.

"I'm on your jury," he said.

"What?"

"Your peer review jury." He shifted uncomfortably. "That thing your mom is doing. She came into my English class asking for volunteers. I signed up, and then I just checked the board and saw that you'd been added to . . . "

"The list of criminals," Sam blurted, finishing his sentence.

He shook his head. "Sam, it was a pretty stupid thing to do."

Tell me about it! she wanted to rave. *Lots of people do stupid things. I'm sure the person who hit Camille was just being stupid.*

She suddenly wanted to blurt the whole truth about the dressing room. She wanted Dylan to know that it hadn't just been her. Jen had done it, too. So, was she right to protect Jen? And what about Jen? Was it really healthy for Jen not to share the blame? And what else had Jen done?

Sam took a breath, wondering if she dare share her secret. She hadn't even talked this over with Kenny. She couldn't. Kenny might blab to his dad or his dad's girlfriend, who was a good friend of her mom's. It was another example of Kenny being too close for comfort.

But there was no chance to share anything else, because Barry interrupted. With his usual lack of social skills, Barry started talking to Dylan about the next phase of the competition, totally unaware that he'd rudely cut Sam off.

Sam stepped back, annoyed at Barry. But then she caught sight of something else and Barry disappeared from her mind. She had just caught a glimpse of Jen, who had slipped out of the nook near Mr. Congdon's room. At the same time, Rafe Danielson was coming out of the music room, where he'd probably gone to change his clothes. He was wearing his track sweats now and carrying his suit. His blond hair almost covered his eyes. Even so, he looked tired.

Jen rushed up to him with a needy, hopeful grin.

To Sam's surprise, Rafe acted like he barely knew Jen. According to Jen, Jen and Rafe had been hot and heavy since the Destruction Dance. Sam hurried over just in time to catch the end of their conversation.

"Sorry, Jen, but I've got to go," Sam heard Rafe say. "I have a test tomorrow."

"Why didn't you ever call me?" Jen pleaded. "Did you just listen to Kristine and all those other people? Is that why you dumped me? Do you think I'm just some slut? Is that why?"

"Jen, I haven't listened to anybody," Rafe insisted. "Can't we just forget this whole thing?"

"I can't forget it," Jen argued. "It's everywhere I go. Nobody else will forget it. I want it to be over. I want it to go away."

Rafe turned away from her.

"Don't do this to me," Jen pleaded.

Without another word, Rafe just walked away.

Sam caught up to Jen just as Rafe escaped and Jen turned toward the wall. "Jen," she said.

Jen pulled away from her. Her eyes looked wild.

"What's going on with you and Rafe?"

Jen spun around. "NOTHING! Can't you tell? I can't stand this any more. I have to stop this. I'm NOTHING!"

"But I thought . . . "

"Don't think, Sam. I don't want to think anymore. I've had enough thinking. I CAN'T DO THIS ANYMORE!" she screamed.

Everyone stared.

"Go home without me," Jen ordered.

Before Sam could say anything else, Jen started to run toward the school's front entrance, down past the library and into the main hall.

"Jen, it's too late to walk!" Sam called. "You know . . . "

Sam stopped mid-sentence. She considered running after Jen, but then she decided to take Jen's advice and just forget it! How much more could she lie for Jen? Should she keep protecting her? And what about Camille? Should she let Camille keep pushing right into a nervous breakdown? Feeling like her two best friends wanted to throw themselves off a cliff, Sam stood for a moment, wondering whether she would fall with them.

That's when Sam saw Dylan again. He seemed to be on his way out. But when he saw Sam just standing there, he actually walked over. He was about to say something. Sam looked at him. Their eyes had actually connected when an incredible sound exploded somewhere else in the school.

CRAAAAAAAASSSSSHHHHHH!

Sam looked around, totally confused. It sounded like the smashing of glass, tinkling then more crashing, like an explosion in the Arctic Circle. For a moment Sam couldn't tell whether it came from the parking lot, from inside the theater or from somewhere in outer space.

Then people began to run. Someone shouted something about the main hall, and everybody else got swept along as if a tidal wave were chasing them. Sam and Dylan ran, too, following the crowd that ran down towards the offices and the main entrance into school.

When Sam got to the main hall, she and Dylan stepped back in shock. A circle of people stood outside the attendance office, staring at the glass display cases that were across the hall.

"Who did this?" Sam gasped.

No one answered.

All they knew was that someone had just smashed one glass door of the athletic trophy case. They'd taken out Rafe Danielson's track trophy and broken it into pieces. An arm rested here. A gold torso had fallen there. A leg that had been reaching for a hurdle, now dangled on the floor like a piece of a discarded doll.

Lastly, the trophy's head had been thrown into the biggest trophy case, splintering so much glass that the whole hallway looked like it had been bombed. It was almost beautiful in a way. The glass shards glittered like angry diamonds all over the floor.

12

RAP . . . RAP . . . RAP . . .

"May we have order please."

The mumbles and chattering swelled like an ocean wave and then receded just as quickly. In the stuffy air of Mr. Hammond's math classroom, chitchat seemed to be everywhere, even though this was the most serious of events—the first West L.A. High peer review.

Tony Goldman, a big bear of a senior, had been appointed presiding officer. He nodded to Alison, who was overseeing the proceedings, which were being held an hour before school even began. It was understood that any judgment and/or punishment would be handed down by students and students alone. Alison was on hand only to guide and consult.

Which made it all the worse for Sam.

Sam squirmed in the chair that had been set out for her at the back of the room. She sat with the other "criminals" who were waiting for their cases to come up. A couple of long tables had been brought in from the science class, and that was where the members of the jury sat—seniors Katie McBride, Johanna Jackson and Bruce Akimoto, plus juniors Joshua Grenrock and . . . Dylan.

Sam didn't want to look at Dylan, but it was impossible to completely avoid him since he was sitting all of fifteen feet away. He was dressed in a white polo shirt, and dark, new-looking jeans. His long legs dangled out to one side and she could see his worn track shoes laced in the West L.A. high school colors. That was a new addition—spirit shoelaces. Sam wondered if they had been provided by Kristine's stupid Social Activities Committee. At least Dylan's red hair looked messy. His eyes seemed pretty unspirited, and his expression said nothing to her.

Sam's stomach felt like it was full of rocks. She wanted to simultaneously shrink under her chair and stand up and shout, *"How dare you judge me? You know nothing about this! You know nothing about any of this, and neither do I!"* But then that was just the beginning of the conflicting, swirling, dizzying craziness that was happening inside of her. She had the strangest sense of dislocation. Her mother was sitting alongside the wall with Vice Principal Sizar, looking as mom-like as a piece of granite. Kids that normally would be bumping, yakking and tugging at her in the hallways, now whispered as if they were waiting on death row.

"I heard they're calling in Ron Claussen next time, to retry him for breaking that window," worried Devon Russell. "They'll give him community service for a year."

"Isn't that against the law?" Pete Thomas mentioned. "Can you really try somebody twice for the same thing?"

Devon thought about it.

It was ironic. Three weeks ago, these two guys had tried to kill each other in front of the cafeteria milk dispenser. Now they were almost acting like friends.

"What about the trophy case? Did they find out who did that?" whispered Betty Kai Lee. "What an incredible mess."

"Whoever did that is a head case," Devon told her.

"But when they find that person," agreed Pete, "that poor sucker's gonna end up in here."

"That sucker will get community service for ten years."

Sam didn't want to think about the trophy case. She refused to think about it, or talk about it. She couldn't believe what she feared might be true.

Maybe it wasn't true, she told herself. It couldn't be. It had to have been someone else.

Sam suddenly pictured the whole student body getting dragged before peer review at one time or another. Maybe they were crazy. The trophy incident just proved that things were out of control. Whoever had done it—and Sam didn't want to think about who that might have been—had to be pretty nuts.

Maybe there was something in the drinking fountains. Sam sure didn't know what kind of insanity had overtaken her in Kristine's dressing room. She didn't know why her normally disciplined and moral self had gotten so weird and primitive. So maybe it could happen to anyone. Maybe any normal student could one day just lose her mind.

Sam glanced over at Kenny, who was sitting among the two dozen yawning spectators. She wondered what he was thinking, but he'd been busy preparing for a jazz band concert, and she hadn't had a chance to talk to him about it. Camille had stayed home for the last few days—on doctor's orders. And Jen, well . . . luckily Jen was avoiding this whole peer review.

Kristine hadn't avoided it. No way. She was sitting between Dawn and Stacy, waiting to see Sam take the hit. About a half dozen more Kristine wannabes sat behind them.

Tony brought down his gavel. They were finishing the review for Caroline Shaw, who sat at the head of the first long table. Usually a perky party girl, Caroline looked weary and ashamed. Sam had also noticed a couple of parents among the spectators, two of whom were obviously Caroline's.

"Okay, we have a verdict for Caroline."

Caroline put her head down.

Tony cleared his throat. "Caroline, you are guilty of bringing and consuming alcohol at a school event. You also encouraged and allowed other students to drink, at the same Friday night dance. Your sentence is as follows . . . "

Caroline took a deep breath.

"You will perform sixteen hours of community service." Tony reached for another piece of paper. Bruce Akimoto whispered in his ear. Tony nodded, then faced Caroline again. "Your community service will be to volunteer at the West L.A. Senior Center. You'll help with free breakfast every Saturday until your time has been served."

Caroline didn't look happy, but she didn't protest. She just signed her service agreement, then padded off with her folks.

"Caroline wasn't the only one who drank at that dance, you know," a spectator called out.

Dawn Warrington shushed him.

Tony slammed down the gavel. "Order, order. If the spectators are not silent, they will be asked to leave."

Sam decided that Tony was getting a little carried away. She was also relieved to hear Caroline's sentence. Sam did community service all the time. She was a regular volunteer at the youth center, and would have worked there—or at the senior center—for the next hundred Saturdays, peer jury or not. She was glad to finally see some kind of silver lining to this review, because she was up next.

"Next case."

The crowd quieted.

Tony looked down at the papers in front of him. "Samantha Crane."

Sam stood up and glanced at her mom, suddenly hoping for a glimpse of sympathy or support. Her mother wouldn't even make eye contact.

Sam took the hot seat at the head of the jury table.

"Samantha, the charges against you are as follows," Tony read. "You trespassed onto school property after hours. You entered the theater dressing room, where you defaced and vandalized both personal and school property. Is that correct?"

"Yes," Sam said in a voice that was totally unfamiliar to her. Dylan was staring at her.

"Do you have anything to say?"

Sam's mind raced. All week she'd agonized over whether or not to tell the truth about Jen. She could think of a dozen reasons why Kristine had deserved it, and a million reasons why she should explain that she hadn't done it alone. At the same time, she flashed on two things that Kenny always said, *Two wrongs don't make a right,* and *Don't be a rat.*

She also thought about the trophy case. After the smashed glass and those broken pieces of Rafe's trophy, she didn't want to drag Jen into anything.

There was a general shuffling in the room, feet nervously moving, a little mumbling and some repositioning in chairs. Sam realized that Tony was waiting for an answer.

Dylan was still staring at her.

Alison intruded. She looked calmly at Sam.

"Samantha, do you want to say anything about what you did?"

Sam swallowed. "No."

It was abrupt. More abrupt then Sam had meant it to be. But she'd promised to protect Jen, and a promise was sacred. Sam also knew in her gut that it would be a major disaster if Kristine found out about Jen. Maybe Jen had already lost her senses, but Sam owed it to her to be loyal nonetheless.

Tony looked compassionate. "Sam, are you sure you don't have anything you'd like to say?"

"I'm sure."

There were further mumbles in the room. Stacy huffed and stormed out. An amazing feeling startled Sam . . . *There are people in this room who hate me so much, and they don't even know who I really am, or what is at stake here!* She also felt guilty and embarrassed. And she hated having Dylan, Kenny and her mom see her in a position like this.

Tony cleared his throat. "Well, Samantha, I'd like to recommend that we consider your outstanding record of student leadership and the concern and responsibility that you have shown at this school. We can't ignore that." He smiled at Alison.

There was a hiss from one of Kristine's followers, plus a few whispers of "rigged," and "unfair."

Tony banged down on the gavel. "If there's more of that, you'll be asked to leave."

Silence. Sam wished it felt better. Out of the corner of her eye she saw her mother stand up.

Alison glanced at Kristine. "I'd like to say something."

"Yes, Officer Crane."

"I don't think a student's past record or achievements should effect the proceedings here. Samantha committed a serious offense, and she needs to take the consequences." Alison folded her arms and sat back down.

Great, just great. Sam felt the most complex mix of shame and rage. On the other hand, she didn't care if she were given ten years of community service. She believed in serving the community. Her whole high school career had been about helping other people. So why was her mother trying to rub it in her face?

The peer jury began discussing the case among themselves. Sam's eyes caught Dylan leaning into the center and stressing a certain point, over and over. Finally the other jurors nodded, and Tony took the floor again.

"Thanks, Dylan," Tony said softly. "Point well taken."

Sam steeled herself. Now both Dylan and her mother were staring at her, as if she were going to be sent to a maximum security lockup. *Fine*, she wanted to yell. *Give me community service for a thousand years, a million years. I'll serve at soup kitchens and wipe noses at Head Start. I'll pick up park litter and tutor sixth graders. I'll do it all. It's okay!*

Tony leaned forward. "Sam, as punishment

for your offense, the jury has decided on the following sentence."

Sam sat up very straight.

"Sam, since your offense did damage to our school, the jury thinks that you should directly help our school." He glanced back at Dylan. "First, you'll be in charge of painting and repairing the spirit sign that was destroyed near the bleachers."

"What?" Sam groaned. The spirit sign? People were going nuts in their school and they wanted her to waste her time painting a spirit sign?

Dylan wrote something on a paper and slid it over to Tony. Dylan had done this to her, Sam realized. He knew that community service wasn't a *punishment* for her. So he came up with the worst kind of service she could imagine.

"And second," Tony continued. He looked down at Dylan's paper and read, "You will provide twenty hours of volunteer time to the Social Activities Committee, helping on any of their projects that might benefit the school."

Applause burst out among the Kristine partisans, but Sam was ready to throw up. Of all the stupid, useless things to make her do! This wasn't going to help anyone or anything. They were selling her into slavery to Kristine. It had been Dylan's idea! And her mother had helped it happen.

Tony banged down on the gavel. "Order," he demanded. "Order . . . Sam, do you accept your sentence?"

"Do I have a choice?" Sam back-talked. "I'm sorry. Yes, I accept," she said. Then she turned away from her mother and Dylan, and walked out of the room.

Alison was alone.

She came out of the classroom feeling like she was in a daze. She felt the weight of her gun under her corduroy blazer. She folded her arms and stopped for a moment, as if to reassure herself that she was the real Alison Crane . . . with a daughter that she loved and had just helped to humiliate.

Alison reeled.

Students passed by. Some stared with curiosity. One girl slowed down, as if she wanted to talk. *Not now,* Alison thought. She ignored them and left campus, running away from the lockers and the thick cafeteria smell and the constant noise.

When she'd started this project she'd felt so hopeful. She'd been riding high over her success with Randy Carelli. She was sure she'd have every teen in the palm of her hand. Every teen except her own daughter, who had only told her a half truth about what she'd done at school and why it had happened.

Before she knew it, Alison was out on Bonita Place. She didn't have a squad car this time. She'd taken the community service car that officers were assigned to use for public relations. Alison wondered if what she'd just done to her daughter would count as the ultimate public relations failure. She remembered girls like Kristine Moore from her own high school days. She'd been snubbed by Kristine's mother and had felt her own insecurity and rage.

Alison opened the car door, but she couldn't get in. She just wanted to know why Sam had done it. And she wanted to know if Sam had really done it alone. She knew that Sam had never liked Kristine, but the dressing room incident was so extreme, so nasty. Maybe Alison had just forgotten what it felt like to be sixteen.

Looking down the street along the edge of campus, Alison thought about Sam and her friends. They all seemed so strained lately. Camille's mother said Camille had even started having nightmares, and that the incident at the Governor's Award speech competition had been considered a flashback or anxiety attack.

That was another thing bothering Alison. Camille. The hit-and-run was Alison's case and she didn't have a clue. Carlos had gone on to other things. Maybe that's why she'd thrown herself into this peer review—to avoid facing a simple case that she hadn't been able to solve.

With that, Alison closed the car door again. She began to pace. Hit-and-run. Theft. Vandalism. Smashing that huge glass trophy case into smithereens. Alison had this overwhelming hunch that all the trouble that had been happening at West L.A. High was connected. It was as if a poison had gotten into the student body's bloodstream. If someone like Sam had gone haywire, then who else was losing his or her mind?

Halfway down Orange Street, Alison looked around. Most students were just arriving at school. A few adults jogged. A cat ran under a parked car. The air was clean, the sun low and bright. Sprinklers waved, except for one lawn where a lady stood on her grass watering with a hose.

Sondra Carelli.

Alison hurried across the street, over the small hill of grass and up to the Carellis' small house. As soon as Sondra Carelli saw Alison, she dropped her hose and slipped in behind her screen door. About thirty-five years old, with stringy brown hair and olive skin, Mrs. Carelli wore only her bathrobe and red flip-flops.

Alison turned off Mrs. Carelli's hose, which was squirting water down the driveway. Then she held out her badge and banged on the screen door. "It's me, Mrs. Carelli. It's Officer Alison Crane. Can I talk to you?"

Two dogs bayed. "Is it Randy?" Mrs. Carelli finally answered. "He went to school. Is he in trouble again?"

"No, it's not about Randy," Alison called. "Can you please come out?"

There was more barking, then Mrs. Carelli pleaded with the dogs. Finally she appeared again, a sweater flapping over her thin bathrobe. There was a bruise below her right eye.

"What is it?" she pouted.

"It's not Randy," Alison offered. "Are you all right?"

"I'm fine," Mrs. Carelli snapped. "I didn't call you. *You* wanted to talk to *me*."

Alison took a moment. "Did Randy tell you that I found out about a computer class at the junior college for him?" she asked. "He's good with computers."

Mrs. Carelli softened a little. "He told me."

"Mrs. Carelli," Alison went on. "I just want to ask you about something that happened two weeks ago, in the street in front of your house. There was a hit-and-run accident that injured a sixteen-year-old African-American girl. This girl has a small build. She's only five-foot-one. Medium-dark skin. Her hair was in cornrows. She was wearing a blazer and leggings."

One of the dogs whined.

"Did you see anything!" Alison pressed. "My partner and I have interviewed all the other people on your block. No one answered your door that night, but I had the feeling someone might have been home. Is there any chance that you might have seen something?"

Mrs. Carelli looked wary.

"Mrs. Carelli, the girl that was hit is just a little bit older than Randy. It could have been Randy, in fact. And this girl might have been killed."

The dog jumped onto the screen, pushing the door open a little.

Alison reached in and touched Mrs. Carelli's arm. "Please help me, Sondra. The girl who was hurt is a very good friend of my daughter's."

Sondra Carelli finally looked at her. "You have a daughter?"

Alison nodded. "If you saw anything, please tell me."

Mrs. Carellis frowned. She brushed hair away from her face, then took a long, deep breath. "Am I in trouble for not answering the door that night?"

"No," Alison assured her. "I don't want to know why you didn't want to talk to me that night. That has nothing to do with the hit-and-run. If you saw anything that has to do with the accident, please tell me now."

Mrs. Carelli glanced up and down the street. She touched her bruise, then let out a long, puffy breath. "Okay, I was out with one of the dogs. I saw the car."

"You did!"

"It sped around the corner from Bonita Place, pretty fast, kind of reckless." Mrs. Carelli looked into the sun and squinted. "Then I heard the brakes, but I didn't realize that someone had been hit until later. By then, other people had arrived to help. My husband, he didn't want me to get involved. He told me not to. He threatened . . . "

Alison didn't make her finish. "I understand. Can you describe the car? Did you really see it? Do you remember what it looked like?"

Mrs. Carelli hesitated. Then she opened the screen door. "I think so," she admitted.

"Thank God," Alison breathed.

Mrs. Carelli glanced around, making sure that no one was coming up the street. "It turned around in our driveway before it sped away again," she whispered. Finally she gestured for Alison to come into the living room.

Alison took out her notebook and walked in. She tried to act calm, even though the adrenaline was rushing through her body. "Please tell me everything you can remember, Mrs. Carelli."

"All right," Mrs. Carelli sighed. For one last time, she peeked out the door, then took a deep breath. "I don't know if it will help, but I'll tell you everything I know."

13

Kristine was having a great day.

"Yee haw," she giggled.

Things had certainly started out on the right foot with Samantha's peer review. Kristine still couldn't believe that Dylan and then Samantha's own mother had basically skewered Sam alive and served her up on a platter.

"Sometimes there is truly justice in the world. Everyone else may think this school is going crazy. I think it's finally becoming sane."

Kristine was on her way to the school library after the final bell. She felt so light and free that her cowboy boots kept scuffing up the black-and-white tiled floor. She rounded the corner near the main offices and passed Ricardo Kahn, a hunky senior football player who was known to date college girls.

"Hi, Kristine," Ricardo flirted. When he

passed, he reached out and caressed her cheek. "Glad to see you smiling again."

"Thanks."

He smiled back, then jogged out towards the gym.

It was amazing. People had been stopping Kristine to ask how she was. Girls had sent poems and notes. Major cute boys had put their arms around her and snuggled. Someone had left a daisy in her locker door, and someone else had put candy hearts on her homeroom desk.

Kristine kicked up her boots again, then had to stop when she walked by the trophy case. What had been glass doors were now covered with cardboard and silver tape. All the trophies had been removed and it really looked awful, one shelf tottering, like a tornado had spun down the middle of the hall. The floor shone in swirls of freshly applied wax, but Kristine could also spot a needle of glass left over, glistening in the corner.

"Sick."

Now that gave Kristine the creeps. Writing mean graffiti was bad enough, but smashing a huge glass cabinet . . . that was scary. That was as scary as that car that hit Camille. People were saying that it was going to get worse. Some kids suspected vandals from rival high schools. They were nervous about that Saturday's track meet, which was against Culver City. Culver kids could be rough, and people feared that someone might get hurt.

It wouldn't be her this time, Kristine was certain. Her enemies were going down. One by one, she had been watching them drop. Jen was a waste of time. Dylan had the shock of discovering Kenny and Sam. Then Camille had had what looked like a psychotic episode during her Governor's Award speech. And Sam had certainly gotten her own that morning at peer review.

Kristine felt indestructible. The stupid play was over. As far as she was concerned, the whole theater could get blown up now. Her Governor's speech was finished. If she won the award—great. And if she didn't win—she didn't need any extra cash for college, so that would be no skin off her behind. They would announce the winner Saturday night, after the big Culver track meet. Kristine didn't care if she never saw another award or leading role or contest again.

"Never again," she gloated.

For the moment, Kristine only wanted to concentrate on two things. First was her cast party, which had grown to include the A-list of the upper-class. And the second thing on Kristine's mind was devising the grossest, grungiest, dumbest social activities tasks that she could assign to Samantha Crane.

"It's only fair." Kristine giggled as she headed to the library to dump off the books she'd used to research Fairness and the Constitution. Stacy had checked them out after Kristine's locker had been raided. Kristine flew through the library doors and dropped her load, letting the books smack down on the librarian's counter.

"Think you could do that any louder," said

someone who was standing at the card catalogue.

Kristine looked over. It was Kenny Sando Wilson, fingering through a file and actually looking cute in big, baggy army pants and a tight black tee shirt.

Kristine smiled at him, then waited to see if he would come over. For some reason, she'd been thinking about him. She'd decided that his bandanna really had brought her luck. He'd been the person to turn the tide for her when she'd hit her all-time low.

But Kenny ignored her. He kept digging through the card file, his light brown skin looking soft and smooth, even under the harsh fluorescent light. Kristine padded past him. No skipping now. With each step, she let her legs get heavier. When she reached the display of new books, she slowly folded down onto the floor, as if all her energy had leaked out.

Sure enough, he slammed his card drawer in and came over. "Are you okay?"

"I'm fine," she answered softly. "I just dropped something."

He put his hand to his slim chest. There was a guitar pick in his hair. "I thought you were like fainting, or something weird like that."

"Me?" Kristine scoffed. Then she pulled her knees up to her chest, gathering her long skirt around her. She inched over until she was between two rows of books, out of sight of the librarian.

Finally Kenny crouched down, too. "Sam told

me about the peer review. So I guess it's all even now."

Not quite, thought Kristine. She kept her eyes on Kenny. Up close, she could study his deep brown eyes, the color of a good wool coat.

Kenny looked away. "But I don't know why she did it. Why Sam did that to you. I mean, I know why, I just don't . . . oh, forget it."

"No, don't forget it," Kristine pressed. She was surprised to feel a surge of genuine anger. "I know what Sam thinks. She thinks my father buys me everything. But I never ask my father to buy me things. I hated doing that play. I knew I was a joke, but my father . . . "

Kenny frowned.

Despite her good mood, Kristine's tears were back. She bit her lip, willing some self-control before any drips ran down her cheeks. "I don't have your bandanna," she spat, embarrassed again. "It's at home. I'll give it back. I promise."

"It's just a bandanna."

Kristine took a long, deep breath, sucking in her tears. "I'm sorry." She looked into his eyes again and suddenly didn't want him to leave. He was comforting like a good coat, too. And warm. "You must think I'm a wreck."

He didn't answer.

"I'm actually doing fine. I really am," she insisted. The librarian walked by and they both huddled. Suddenly Kristine was aware of sitting close to Kenny. Really close. She could smell some kind of soap and she could hear him breathe. For some reason, her own breathing had started to speed up.

"So did you find it?" he asked, after a long pause.

"What?" Kristine whispered.

"Whatever you dropped. Whatever you were looking for."

"Yes. No," Kristine corrected. "It doesn't matter."

Kenny looked totally confused. But he didn't move away.

"You know, I'm planning this party for Friday night," Kristine mentioned. "Maybe it's gotten too huge. I don't know."

He shrugged.

"Would you want to come?" she heard herself say. A month before, he would have been the last person on her list. But now she really wanted to see him there. "You could bring your guitar. Or some music you really like." She felt herself blush. "I'll give you back your bandanna."

Kenny looked unsure.

"It's going to be a huge party, not just my little clique. If you don't want to stay long, you won't have to. It's no big deal."

He stood up and kind of backed off, as if he were slightly afraid of her.

"You don't have to come," she added. "I just wanted to do something nice, to thank you for being nice to me the other day. That's all."

Kenny just kept backing up until he almost tripped over a chair. Finally he stumbled past and disappeared behind another shelf of books.

Kristine pulled out a big book about Alaska. She stared into it and started to giggle. Kenny. Kenny at her party. She hoped he showed up. She didn't know what she was going to do if he did show up. She just knew that she wanted to find out.

"Tacos, taquitos, tostados . . . "

"What?"

Sam closed her eyes. She knew her mother was staring at her. They were standing in line, waiting for a table at a local Mexican restaurant, El Tapatio. The festive crepe paper and balloons, the hanging papier-mâché, bulls and demons, the kids going by with noisemakers and party hats, the families, all of this reinforced a kind of weary goofiness in Sam, like she'd been pummeled in her brain.

Her mother didn't get it. "Are you hungry?"

"I guess."

"It shouldn't take too long."

Sam shifted and nervously jiggled her foot. As a gesture of reconciliation, her mom had insisted that they go to their favorite Mexican restaurant from eons ago. Sam had loved it here when she was a little girl. She still loved it—the mariachi music coming over the corny little PA system, the waitresses with their hair in spit curls, tottering on high heels, but still balancing trays of icy green margaritas. Sam even liked the waiting line. She could stand there and watch ESPN flash across the upper corner television, pro football players tackling each other to the theme of Mexican music. Then a tray filled with burritos, beans, rice and chili rejenos, plus something spicy with cayenne and cinnamon went by. Sam's nose wanted to unlatch from her head and just follow along.

Yeah, she was in a weird mood all right.

But it wasn't good weird, it was creepy weird. Edgy and worried and nuts. The kind of weird that could turn into horrendous tears and unstoppable fury. After her trial that morning, Sam didn't know if she'd ever feel good weird again.

And creepy weird felt even creepier, because her mother wasn't her mother anymore. At least not her recognizable mother. Sure, her mom brought her to the old restaurant, and she was passing along furtive, hinting smiles, like everything was okay and she hadn't meant to abandon Sam in front of Kristine and Dylan. And now they were supposed to eat the old comfort food and be comfortable again.

Right.

"Your table is ready."

A waitress came up with a bright smile and cheeks so fresh and scrubbed Sam wanted to reach out and scratch them. She couldn't imagine what her mother had in mind for this dinner. What were they going to talk about? It was pathetic, Sam thought, as she watched her mother walk through the restaurant, stiff and purposeful, like somebody who had done something really hurtful, and was now trying to pretend that it hadn't happened.

Sam felt a sense of martyred power. Maybe she was getting to her mom. Maybe the happy childhood memories were making her mother realize how badly things had deteriorated, and how no amount of nostalgia was going to bring it back. They hiked past several messy, happy families, squeezed by other waiters, and listened to the fajitas sizzling in cast-iron pans.

When they found their place, Sam didn't bother touching the chips or the crayons. She just sat in the straight-backed wooden chair and stared at her mom.

Alison pushed back her hair and bit her lip. "I'm sorry about the peer review, Sam."

Sam let out a stream of hot breath. She sounded like a dragon.

"But you had it coming. I'm still not sure you told the whole truth, but it's over."

"Right." Sam thought for a moment. "Maybe it's over for you."

"I had to make sure that I wasn't favoring you."

"I think everybody was impressed by your professional detachment." Sam reached ahead and grabbed the basket of tortilla chips. She stuck one in her mouth like a two-year-old and munched down. She truly was losing her mind.

Alison cringed and then looked disgusted. Sam opened her mouth up, fully aware of the half-munched tortilla she was displaying. "Would you like some?" she asked, sounding more like a cow than a human. She hadn't done this since she was about eight. She wondered what she would do next. Stand on the table? Strip off all her clothes?

Her mother shook her head with disdain. Sam plopped the basket back down and kept eating.

"Are you ready to order?" A handsome, dark-haired young man in his early twenties was leaning down between the two of them. His hands were on pen and order tablet, and his waist was sashed in red. Sam felt like a bull who'd just seen a cape.

"Yes," Sam said.

Her mother's eyebrows raised. "We're not ready yet," she intruded. "Could you give us some more time?"

The waiter looked confused.

Sam slapped a flat palm down into the table. She wondered what her mother would do if she ordered a beer. She decided not to find out. "Could you bring me a Diet Coke?"

He turned to Alison. "For you, Señorita?"

"A beer. Dos Equis, please." Alison put her elbows across the table and leaned down over it and glared at her daughter.

The gesture was right out of a forties movie and it suddenly struck Sam as absurd. The waiter, who must have thought he'd won the psychotic women's table, scurried away, mumbling under his breath. Mariachis were in range and they were playing those huge guitars that were large enough to house a Labrador retriever.

"Look Sam, obviously you're angry at me, and you're acting like you're in second grade. In any case, I have something important to talk to you about."

Sam licked her fingers.

"I finally made some progress on Camille's case," Alison said in a professional tone of voice. She took off her glasses, revealing tired, worried eyes. "I found a witness today. I need your help."

Sam was stunned. She'd thrown her worst at her mother, and still her mom was together enough to come back with this. On her mom's first few cases, all Sam had wanted was to get involved. It had been a constant battle to keep Sam out of Alison's police work. And now her mother was actually coming to her for help?

But what kind of help did her mother want? What was her mother going to ask Sam to reveal?

"I finally found a witness this morning," Alison repeated. "I talked to one of the neighbors who saw a car speed off right after Camille's accident. She gave a good description of the car. A very good description . . . "

"What did you find out?" Sam blurted.

"It's a late model sedan. A dark color."

"Great," Sam scoffed. "That only sounds like five million cars in L.A."

"I know. The witness saw the car pull into her driveway and turn around. She didn't see the driver, but she thought that the car had come out of the parking lot at the high school, meaning that it was likely to have been driven by a West L.A. High student."

Sam sat up. Someone from school had hit

Camille? Someone from West L.A. High? No, please, no . . .

"That's where I need your help, Sam. See if you recognize any of these details from cars you might see in the parking lot at school," Alison stated. She began her list. "There was a dent on the side of the front fender. Something was laying behind the back seat, almost blocking the rear window—which may have made it hard for the driver to see—and there was a sticker on the back bumper that said, "Student of the Month, Rosedale Elementary."

Sam felt sick. The music felt like a wooden board smacking at her head. All she could think was, *NO, NO, NO, NO!*

"Does that ring a bell, Sam? Do you know whose car that was?"

Sam willed her face to remain expressionless. Her insides were going crazy. That was Jen's mother's car! Sam had no doubt. Sam had been with Jen a few months before when Jen had rammed into a pole outside Mrs. Gooches's Market. Sam remembered the stack of jackets piled up in the back window when Jen had driven her to the dance—in fact, she'd noticed that the view was blocked and had thought about taking the jackets down. Sam had noticed the Rosedale Elementary bumper sticker, too. Jen's mom had put it on, and then Jen had ripped it off a few days after the dance. Not only that, but Jen had left the dance early—at least Sam thought she had.

The more Sam thought about it, the more

awfully it all fit together. Jen had trashed Kristine's dressing room, so why couldn't she have stolen the books, too? And then there was the spirit sign. And the trophy case, of course. Rafe Danielson's trophy had been the target, and it had happened right after Rafe had told Jen to get lost.

Sam's brain felt like it was going to explode. Despite the evidence, she told herself that she might be wrong. She had to be wrong! Jen wasn't the type to steal. Jen wouldn't get back at Rafe by smashing a school glass cabinet. Camille was Jen's best friend. There were a zillion dark sedans in L.A. Everybody got into fender benders. And every month somebody new got a bumper sticker from Rosedale Elementary . . .

"Sam, do you recognize the car I described?"

Sam refused to answer. She didn't want to recognize any of it. She didn't want to rat on her best friend. She didn't want to give evidence that might make this nightmare turn into truth.

There had to be doubt. Sam would find some shred of doubt. She still couldn't believe that Jen had done it. She wouldn't believe it, even though the evidence was beginning to scream inside her head. Would Sam be an accessory if she didn't speak up? Sam didn't want to know. She didn't want to know if a chat over tortillas with her mother counted as an official police inquiry.

"Sam, what are you thinking? Do you know anything about this? Do you have a hunch, an idea?"

"NO!" Sam lied. Her voice has risen above

the level of the mariachi music. She didn't care. Jen was her best friend. Maybe it was part of her mother's campaign to humiliate her for the mistake with Kristine. Maybe her mom knew that Jen had been in on that, too, and this was just a trap. Then again, maybe Jen *had* done it all—the spirit sign, the book theft, the trophy case, the hit-and-run.

"Sam, do you have any idea who that car belongs to!" Alison repeated.

"Of course I don't know!" Sam ranted. She wouldn't rat on Jen. She couldn't. If Jen had practically killed Camille, and then just driven away, then Sam's whole world was upside down. Nothing could make any sense if that were true.

"Sam."

"And I really resent you asking me to get involved in this after the way you treated me this morning at the peer review. I'm not supposed to get involved in your cases, remember!"

"Sam."

"I don't deserve any special treatment, remember?"

"SAM."

"I'm not responsible or special, remember!"

"Sam, I never said that!"

"I'm not even grown-up enough to do normal community service for my crime. I have to be handed over to stupid Kristine to do stupid, useless things at school." Sam stood up. Her hands flew out, and the basket of tortilla chips fell to the floor. "If I deserve that, what makes you think I can remember somebody's stupid bumper sticker or figure out who almost killed Camille!"

"Sam, calm down. Think about it."

"No, you calm down. You think about it." Sam couldn't stop. She'd found a way out of answering her mother's questions and there was no going back now. "How can I help you solve a serious crime, when maybe my crime was just as serious! I DON'T KNOW WHY YOU BOTHER TO ASK ME ANYTHING!" she screamed.

Now it was Alison who looked sick. Sam didn't care. She didn't care about the people staring at her. The kids, the balloons, the mariachis, the happy-faced waiters . . . she pushed past all of them, then flew out the door and began running up La Brea Avenue.

Sam raced along the sidewalk, almost running into a woman with a stroller and a old lady using a cane. She figured that her mom would try and follow, but she wasn't going to ride home with her. She wasn't going to speak to her mother until this was settled. She was either going to figure this out or she was going to crack up.

Unless she already had . . .

14

It wasn't helping.

Everything just made it worse.

Smash. Grab. Black out.

In the moment, that split second of action, it had some purpose. But as soon as it was over, the feeling was just darker and more empty. The first mistake just looked sicker and bigger. It was all going to end soon. There was no other way.

Coming after me . . . coming after me.

The reason was finally clear.

Trying to even the score didn't help.

Hurting things didn't help.

The one person who really needed to be hurt was still walking around, smiling, fooling them all.

Why hadn't it been clear before?

That one person had the secret.

That one person was the cause of all this pain.

* * *

"I feel like those gardeners in *Alice in Wonderland.*"

"What do you mean?"

"The ones that screwed up the flowers on the trees and had to paint them the right color for the queen. I wonder if they thought they were losing their minds."

Camille stared at Sam. "I don't think they painted the queen's roses blue and gold."

"I know," Sam answered. "Red and white, or white and red. Maybe I *don't* know. Everything is so mixed up. I don't know anything anymore. Just throw me down the rabbit hole and watch me break my neck."

On Friday afternoon, Camille felt like she had finally woken up from her *Alice in Wonderland* nightmare. It had been her first day back at school, since her breakdown at the Governor's Award speech. It had also been her first chance to find Sam. Until then, she'd been busy getting back homework assignments and taking make-up tests.

Even so, Camille had survived all seven periods, and now she was still surviving, even though it was almost dinnertime. The track meet against Culver was coming to a close, and Sam was completing the first of her punishment tasks—repainting the spirit sign.

The person who didn't look like she was surviving was Sam. As much as Camille was feeling sane again, Sam looked like she was ready for the loony bin.

"At least you're back in school." Sam dipped

her paintbrush and went over the school logo. She'd already repainted the whole rectangle white. Now she was filling in the letters, which had been outlined for her by someone from Advanced Art.

"Yeah. Today went pretty well," Camille agreed. She was ecstatic to be back in school, even though she had to admit that she'd needed the rest. For the first few days home, she'd slept and slept. Then she'd just spaced out, watching videos and reading comic books. She'd never let herself flake out like that before.

The doctor had explained her problem. He'd called it "flooding," getting overwhelmed by competing stimuli, combined with a little memory loss. It was all caused by the accident, he'd said, and would gradually go away. But even with what they'd called a "closed head injury," Camille could only sit still for so long.

"I dropped out of the Governor's Award contest," Camille told Sam. She neatened Sam's paint job with her purple fingernail.

Sam looked surprised. That was the first big reaction Camille had gotten out of her. Sam seemed so jumpy and weird. If Camille hadn't known better, she'd have guessed that Sam was the one with swelling on the brain.

"I couldn't have won anyway, girlfriend. Not with a big zero for twenty percent of the score." Camille winked. "Don't worry, that's the only reason I dropped out. I'm still the same old Camille."

"Oh."

Camille stretched out on the bleacher bench. The meet was almost over, and the crowd had thinned. The Culver kids were leaving, too. Despite expectations of trouble, it had been a pretty mellow event.

"They still want me to come to the awards dinner tomorrow night." Camille shook her cornrows. "I guess I'll grace them with my presence."

Sam didn't laugh. "I'll be there, too," she grunted. "As the waitress. Maybe not even the waitress. Since Kristine is in charge, I'll probably be the dishwasher. The floor scrubber. The toilet bowl cleaner. I don't care." She messed up some of her painting. "I don't care about anything anymore."

"Wait a minute," Camille objected. "What is going on here? I know being Kristine's servant isn't any fun, but you can take it." Camille sensed that Sam was totally strung out. She tried to joke nonetheless, "Well, don't worry. I'm sure Kristine won't win the award."

Sam wiped her brow, leaving a smear of blue paint. "Who will?" she barked. "Who cares."

"You do. I do," Camille blabbed. "Maybe Suria. I heard she aced her swim meet."

"Dylan just won the race today," Sam said sadly. Her voice caught. "Did you see it?"

Camille nodded. Maybe that was it. Maybe Sam was still moping over Dylan. But even Sam didn't usually get this distraught over boys. "Is that what's bothering you, girlfriend? Is it Dylan? Hey, where's Kenny? Not to change the subject. Actually I think it's kind of the same subject—Dylan and Kenny."

"Camille!" Sam cried.

"What?" Camille waved her hands. "Lighten up, Sam. What's bothering you?"

"Nothing," Sam accused. "Everything. You haven't been in school for the last few days. You don't know how weird this place is starting to feel. You don't know what's been going on here. And I'm not the one pushing myself too hard," Sam snapped.

"No, but you're part of the weirdness around here, I can tell you that," Camille muttered. "Besides, I'm not pushing myself. Not today, anyway. I've been given a clean bill of health. I can even go out tonight. If I'm not too tired. Just in time, too."

"What for?"

"Kristine is having some huge party," Camille sighed. "Jen wants to go, just to show that she's not a complete wimp. But of course, she won't go alone. Anyway, I said I'd go with her."

Sam had stopped painting. "Jen is going to Kristine's party?"

"Just to show her face."

Sam took in a huge gulp of air, then collapsed over her thighs. "I can't stand it anymore."

"What?"

Sam let out a little sigh, then a gasp and a moan. She put her hands to her face, streaking her face with blue paint until she looked like someone from another planet. Camille immediately hugged her, smearing blue paint all over her African print dress.

"I'm getting you all blue," Sam said, weeping and sputtering. "I'll stop crying. I'm fine. I'm sorry . . ."

Camille held her. A few of Kristine's spirit groupies marched by, obviously checking on Sam. Camille protected her. When they were finally gone, she asked, "What is going on?"

Sam shuddered. "My mom finally talked to a witness that saw the car that hit you."

"What!" Now Camille felt some panic of her own. All day she'd been feeling so calm. She'd still forgotten a few words here and there, but she hadn't had a cow about it. Even so, mentioning the accident brought back her jangly terror. "Did they find the driver?"

Sam bit back tears. Her face and hands were completely smeared with blue paint. "The witness didn't say anything about the driver. My mom just gave me the description of the car."

"And?"

"I didn't tell my mother . . . but the car that hit you . . . it was Jen's mom's Nissan." Sam heaved another sob, then turned to hide her face.

Camille felt like she'd been knocked in the head again. Sam's information was physically painful and she could feel her heart start to race. "I thought I just dreamed it," Camille blurted. "The last few days, flashes have been coming back. And that's what I've been seeing. Like these bits of light. Images. The front bumper. The headlights. That's the hardest to remember. The lights. It's Jen's car that I've been seeing. Oh God. I mean, Jen's mom's car."

Sam grabbed Camille's wrists with her trembling, blue hands. "My mother will find out soon. I didn't tell her, but it won't take her long to figure it out."

Camille blinked. She was seeing it again. A glare. A flash. A blinding moment of metal, and the screech of the brakes. The rest of it was like some memory from when she was four years old. It was so dim and uncertain.

"Are you sure it was Jen's car!" Sam pleaded.

"I think it was," Camille heaved. She didn't want to remember. It just made her head swim and her breathing get so shallow that her chest hurt. "But I'm not sure."

"You're not?"

"Not positively. Maybe I'm crazy. Maybe it's just wishful thinking. Maybe I just can't face the fact that my best friend would do something like that. But it's also something else."

"What?"

"It's so hard," Camille rambled. "I remember these little bits, and then they don't fit together. Just when I think it makes sense, none of it seems right. I only know . . . I only know . . . "

"What, Camille? What do you know! Tell me. Please!"

"I know that it was Jen's car," Camille swore.

Sam started to weep again.

Camille grabbed her. "But I really don't think that the driver was Jen."

That night Sam stared at Jen. Jen had come to pick Sam up in her mother's Nissan: the car. Sam glanced around, as if there would be signs everywhere. She half-expected blood stains or telltale marks. *This is the vehicle. This car knows all the secrets. Why won't it talk to me!*

But of course, it was just a car. A boring Japanese sedan that Jen's mother drove to Ralph's Market and to her part-time job at an accounting firm. The car seemed very clean. The coats were no longer piled up behind the back seat. The student-of-the-month bumper sticker had been peeled off, even though a faint rectangle of glue remained. The fender still had its obvious dent, but the dark paint gleamed with wax and the windshield sparkled.

"Thanks for subbing for Camille," Jen said to Sam. She drummed the clean steering wheel, then carefully pulled out of the alley next to Sam's apartment building. She waited to turn onto Spaulding Avenue.

Sam folded and unfolded her hands. "I didn't want to stay home with my mom," she responded truthfully. Since the fight at El Tapatio, and Sam's two-mile solo jog home, Sam and her mom had barely spoken. It was ironic, but driving to Kristine's house was actually preferable to staying home with Officer Alison. Besides, Sam would stay in the car while Jen put in her ten minutes of face time at Kristine's big bash.

"Camille thought she was going to be Wonder Woman again," Sam mentioned. She stared at Jen, looking for clues. "But then she felt pretty tired after her first day back at school."

Jen didn't react, and Sam didn't elaborate. She knew that the gut-wrenching chat on the bleachers had wiped Camille out. "I'm glad Camille decided to take it easy," Sam added.

"Well, thanks for not deserting me."

"I'd never desert you," Sam promised. Her voice caught.

Jen actually smiled. Her eyes were still sad and nervous, but she'd obviously worked hard at displaying the old Jen beauty. Her blond hair had been washed and crimped with some kind of fancy curling iron. Her dress, a floral flowing thing with countless tiny pleats, looked new. At her best, Jen was one of the most beautiful girls in the junior class. And that night, she was looking her best again. If Jen had committed all those crimes at school, she'd suddenly entered a new phase of her lunacy.

"Where was Kenny?" Jen asked. She gave a quick glance back at Sam's apartment building, then drove up Spaulding towards Melrose Avenue.

"He must have been rehearsing with the jazz band again." Sam felt like she was making excuses for everyone! She and Kenny hadn't exactly been on intimate terms over the last couple of weeks, and Sam wasn't sure why. She'd seen Kenny earlier that day, but he'd been in a rush, and she'd been a blue-painted wreck. She had asked about plans for that night, but he hadn't really answered her. She knew that Kenny was rehearsing for a jazz concert. Could there be something else going on?

Sam didn't think so, and she couldn't concentrate on Kenny right then. She could only think about Jen. She was going to tell Jen everything, to confront her friend and find out the truth. She was waiting for the perfect time, even though she knew that there was never a perfect time. For anything. Reminding herself of that, Sam decided just to go for it. She'd blurt everything and see how Jen reacted.

"I just want to show my face at this party," Jen said as she cruised towards Crescent Heights. The streetlights cut her lovely face in half. "I spent an hour before I drove to your place, just psyching myself into this. I think that night that I lost it with Rafe was a turning point. I realized that I'd gotten pretty far down there, and it was time to start working my way back up."

"Really?"

Jen tossed back her crimped hair. "I saw that therapist again—the one I talked to after the movie fiasco. I think I can handle this tonight. I just want ten minutes at this party. That's all I'm asking of myself."

"Good for you."

Jen went on. "I just want them all to know

that I'm still alive and kicking. I don't want to talk to Rafe, or Kristine or Dawn. I just want them to know that I'm not going away. I'm not going to stop trying out for plays. I can handle being dumped. I'm certainly not going to kill myself." Jen glanced at Sam, her beautiful eyes looking clear and determined. There was no vodka bottle in her hand, no fury in her face. She looked like the old beautiful, tentative, slightly sad Jen.

Sam couldn't do it. She couldn't confront Jen just yet. She couldn't ruin Jen's showing at this party, not after Jen had worked so hard to get herself here. Jen was only going to stay for ten minutes. Sam would wait until after the party to confront her about the hit-and-run, the trophy case and the rest.

Jen wove up the canyon that led to Kristine's house, a wide, modern thing lit up like a hotel. It was a jumble of geometric blocks, with windows in varying shapes. There wasn't a parking space for a block in either direction. They could hear the music, the pool splashing and laughter. There was actually a search light in front of the house—like the kind used at movie premieres.

Jen parked. She started to climb out, then turned and grabbed Sam's wrist. "Come with me," she begged.

Sam wasn't dressed for a party. She'd scrubbed her face raw getting rid of the blue paint, and she was afraid that she'd spit in Kristine's perfect face. But then she looked back at Jen.

"It's only ten minutes," Jen urged.

"If I go with you, will you promise to tell me the truth about anything I ask you after we leave? Do you promise!"

Jen looked surprised. And a little confused. "Of course," she answered, as if it were unnecessary to make the deal.

Sam climbed out without a word. Jen didn't say anything either. They both climbed the steep canyon road and walked up to the brightly lit house.

When they reached the door, Sam was blasted with music and light. She spotted Dylan out of the corner of her eye. He was awkwardly moving to the beat and stuffing his face with chips. Sam had the urge to run up to him, but then glanced down at her overall cut-offs, paint-spattered Doc Martens and the old stretched-out sweater she'd borrowed from her mom. She was keeping a low profile at this party. Very low. She'd proved her loyalty to Jen. She'd proved it a hundred times. On Kristine's turf, she needed to look out for number one.

"You're on your own," Sam whispered. "I'm not dressed for this party. I'll meet you back out in the car in ten minutes." Before Jen could object, Sam rushed to find the nearest guest bathroom and locked herself in.

The bathroom had Mexican tile in the shape of leaping dolphins and stunk from orange and rose sachet. There were little initialed guest towels and a fancy-looking toilet with pink balloons hanging from the handle. But mostly, it was just an overly perfumed bathroom, done up for party guests. Sam sat on the edge of the tub and stared at her antique watch.

Two minutes passed. Sam checked her hands. Her nails were still rimmed with blue paint. Blue was imbedded in the creases of her palms. Finally she stood up and looked into the mirror, which was lit with a circle of tiny, pink light bulbs. Sam couldn't believe what it illuminated. Blue was smushed along her hairline. There was a huge purple smudge on one cheek. How had she even left her apartment looking like this?

Sam checked her watch again. At least she'd make use of her time. What else was she supposed to do with her remaining seven minutes? So she opened the deco medicine cabinet and looked for some kind of cleanser.

She was just reaching for a bottle of face lotion, when she saw a blood red envelope stuck in the back of the medicine cabinet. Sam wondered if the envelope could contain hair nets or powder. Maybe it held a prescription or an exotic beauty secret.

"I don't think so," Sam whispered. The envelope looked so odd, stowed behind the tonics and the hair mousse, as if someone had left it there as a secret message that they didn't want found right away.

Sam touched the envelope and it tumbled out. She caught it just before it fell into the toilet bowl.

Please read, it said. The handwriting was tense but neat.

To everyone at West L.A. High—

Now Sam wondered if this was part of some stupid party game. Heck. She was someone at West L.A. High. She stuck her finger in the envelope flap and started to open it.

BLANG BANG!

Someone was smacking the bathroom door with their fist.

"You gonna spend all night in there?" a girl giggled.

"I gotta pee!" a boy called out.

Amidst more laughter, Sam slipped the envelope in her pocket and hurried out. She was immediately hit with the party noise again, the giggles and the light. Not looking at anyone she found a wide staircase that looked like it led to a basement rec room. Sam trotted down, hoping that the downstairs also had a door that led back out to the street.

At the bottom of the stairs Sam heard music again. But this was different, not the loud stuff that was thumping out by the pool. This tune was slow and bluesy. Sam recognized the sound and moved toward it. As she turned the corner and glanced into what was indeed a basement rec room, she realized why the music was familiar. Kenny had played it for her only a few weeks earlier.

"What?" Sam breathed.

Kenny himself was crouching down in front of Kristine's basement CD player, listening in that careful way of his. Sam had to blink to believe that it was really him! He looked almost elegant in a black turtleneck, army surplus pants and boots. His eyes were closed and his lean body swayed slightly to the tune.

Sam couldn't put it together when Kristine moved into her line of vision. Wearing white silky pajamas, the hostess glided like some kind of angel. Ha ha. The nasty, blond angel floated over until she was kneeling next to Kenny.

Sam felt like she was hallucinating. Why would Kenny even be at Kristine's house? Who had invited him? Even when Kristine stood up and slowly pulled Kenny to his feet, Sam felt like she was watching a movie. That's it. Everyone at school had gone loony tunes. Now she was watching an actress playing Kristine Moore. The fake Kristine was slipping her arms around the narrow waist of the impersonator pretending to be Sam's Kenny.

It had to be two fakes, because now Kenny and Kristine were starting to dance. It was a slow dance, with Kristine leaning her head on Kenny's shoulder, and Kenny wrapping his arms around Kristine's silky back. Then Kristine pulled back. She tossed her French braid and smiled at Kenny. She put her manicured hand on his cheek, gave a non-angelic giggle, then pressed her mouth lightly to his neck.

WAIT! Sam wanted to scream. STOP. REWIND. RETAKE. START OVER. Kristine was still kissing Kenny's neck! Sam's world had been turned upside down. Sam wanted to wretch, but she didn't make a sound. She watched as Kenny pulled back for a second, as if he weren't sure what was going on.

That's it, Kenny, Sam wanted to cheer. *Laugh at her. Tell her off! Make one of your classic Kenny monster faces. Cross your eyes and stick straws up your nose.*

But Kenny didn't do any of those things. He ran a hand through his afro and took a short, shaky breath. Catching him off guard, Kristine leaned in fast and kissed his mouth. He staggered. As Kristine murmured, he let her press herself against him, then pulled her in close to kiss her back, again and again.

15

To everyone at West L.A. High:

If you even remember me as a friend, please read this. Please know that I'm sorry. For everything. I never meant to hurt anyone. Please understand.

I once had a friend in fourth grade. We had a tree house, high in her backyard. Up in the tree house one time, we had a fight. It wasn't a bad fight, it just got out of control. I didn't push. She was trying to break off a tree branch to hit me, and she fell. She fell so hard, cracked her head open. Blood. So much blood, running down her face and soaking her white shirt. I wanted to get help, but I was so scared. So I just hid.

A month or so later, my friend moved away. I knew why. Her parents wanted to take her away from me, because I'd hurt her. They thought I would hurt her again. My parents were so angry.

They didn't speak to me for a month. A whole month, without a single look or a word.

I wouldn't have hurt her.

I didn't mean to hurt her.

But now the only way out may be to hurt more people.

I guess I don't care anymore.

I have to do something soon.

Because the only person I ever wanted to hurt was me.

Sam hadn't slept. Her eyes stung. Her head throbbed. Her limbs felt like someone had filled them with concrete.

Even so, she shuffled around the back of the cafeteria, serving her sentence as a cafeteria slave. A hairnet covered her short red hair. It felt like it was holding in her brain. Otherwise, Sam's thoughts might have splattered all over the walls.

Did Jen do it?

If she didn't, who did?

Why did Kenny betray me?

In the meantime, Sam was doing her dirty duty. A tray of dishes filled her arms. She wore her cut-off overalls. In fact, she hadn't changed her clothes at all since the party the night before. The red envelope was still in her pocket. Sam had read it that morning, during her first break from the Governor's Award kitchen duty. The words kept running through Sam's head.

"I don't care anymore. The only way out . . . "

Sam was feeling so disconnected. From her mother. From Jen. From Kenny. When Sam thought about Kenny and Kristine she felt like throwing herself on the floor, kicking and screaming like a two-year-old. She almost felt as if she could have written that horrible letter herself.

But of course, Sam hadn't written that letter. Not even as a joke. And Sam was sure that the letter was no joke. It certainly wasn't part of any party game either. So what was it? Who had written it? Why had it been stowed in Kristine's medicine cabinet?

"I should have read it right away," Sam muttered as she dumped her dirty dishes into the deep cafeteria sink. She pulled down the faucet, which reminded her of a shower head, and sprayed incredibly hot water. The steam stung her eyes. Her hands were encased in rubber gloves, but the heat soaked in anyway and made her want to cry.

Sam knew why she hadn't read the letter right away. After stumbling across Kenny and Kristine, she'd forgotten everything else. Now she knew how Dylan had felt, and why he could barely speak to her. If Jen hadn't been driving, Sam wouldn't have been able to find her way home. So she still hadn't confronted Jen about the hit-and-run. She still hadn't shared any insights with her mom. She still wasn't any closer to the truth.

The steam enveloped Sam, making her feel even more unreal. She was so tired. She wanted to go to sleep, and wake up when this bad movie was over, when everyone was sane again. Sam's movie seemed even worse than the creepy porn film that Jen had almost posed for. As far as Sam was concerned, the Kenny/Kristine story was even more obscene. The only thing worse was the real-life saga about who hit Camille.

As Sam continued to wash the dishes, her whole body felt like the life had been steamed out of it. So far, she'd peeled and boiled onions for French onion soup. She'd grated cheese until her fingertips were raw. She'd rolled chicken in bread crumbs. She'd mopped the kitchen floor. Twice. And she'd taken out every load of garbage, including one that had been snuck back in, just so that Sam could lug it out again.

Between the letter and the grunt work, plus the shock of Kenny and Jen, Sam decided that she was in a prison movie. Or just plain prison. She didn't speak to her fellow inmates—also known as Kristine's spirit saints. She certainly wasn't going to speak to Kristine, who'd wandered in and out only a few times, glancing at Sam and acting smug. After seeing Kristine and Kenny the night before, Sam feared that she might go for Kristine's throat and be put in solitary confinement for the rest of her life.

"Sam, did you start cooking the noodles!"

"Sam? Will you please come and clean this up?"

"Where's Samantha!"

Sam turned the hot water on even harder,

hoping to drown out the voices of Dawn and Stacy and the rest of Kristine's little clones who were all out in the new part of the cafeteria, dressed to the nines, pinning up decorations and setting out the delicate little place settings. The Governor's Award finalists and guests were due to arrive any minute. Within an hour, the winner would finally be announced.

"I think Suria will win," chatted Stacy De Fonte as she held open the swinging door.

Dawn joined her. "Or Dylan. Or maybe Kristine. Please, please, please."

"People are saying that Barry is out. Zero personality points," Stacy gossiped. "And Rafe needed to win that track meet yesterday if he was going to win."

"Camille might have aced it, if she hadn't flipped out."

Tee-hee, tee-hee.

Giggle, giggle, giggle.

"Well, we'll find out soon enough. Hey, somebody needs to take out this garbage again!"

"Where's Sam?"

Sam crouched down, hiding behind a stainless steel shelf.

"SAMANTHA!"

Sam wasn't sure if she was Cinderella or Public Enemy Number One. She'd only served about half of her sentence, but she was tempted to try a jail break. She considered taking the nozzle of steaming water and pointing it at Dawn. She wondered what would happen if she dumped a vat of boiling noodles on the floor.

"Whoa," she told herself. "You are out of control, Crane. Take a break."

"SAM!"

"PEOPLE ARE STARTING TO ARRIVE. WE NEED TO GET RID OF THIS BAG OF GARBAGE. SAM!"

Ignoring her torturers, Sam peeled off her rubber gloves. She remembered the only place where she could find solitude, and snuck back into the cafeteria pantry. Like the rest of West L.A. High, half the cafeteria was renovated and half was falling apart. The pantry was an eight by ten walk-in wooden closet, filled with industrial-sized containers of ketchup, instant potatoes, canned soup, refried beans, tuna fish and mayonnaise. Sam sat on a plastic vat of dishwasher soap and peeled off her hair net. She stared at the clothes she'd stowed in there, her waitress black pants and a white shirt her mom usually wore on shift. She rubbed her eyes with red hands. She remembered Kenny and Kristine, then felt her back pocket and thought about that letter again.

Sam sat like that until she heard the rat-tat-tat of high heels storming their way through the kitchen.

"The royalty has returned," Sam muttered. She hadn't even turned the light on, and in fact she liked sitting there in the dark. She slowly began to change her clothes, ignoring the voices out in the kitchen.

"Where did she go?" Kristine demanded. "Where's Samantha Crane?"

"Sam? Where are you?"

"I thought she was here."

Sam suddenly recognized the voice of Ms. Sanford, the teacher who was running the Governor's Award contest. Sam scrambled to button her white blouse. She would have to reappear soon.

"SAM!" Ms. Sanford yelled.

"I thought she was back here. I hope she didn't leave," Kristine whined. "She's supposed to serve dinner. We're going to start any second."

"Kristine, just go back out to the cafeteria and greet people," Ms. Sanford said in a surprisingly patronizing voice. "I think this might be more important than who's going to serve dinner. Tell Officer Crane that I'm going to check the parking lot. Maybe Sam just stepped out there."

Officer Crane!

Sam froze. What was her mother doing here?

The next voice belonged to Alison. "Jen, just stay here. I'm going out back to look for Sam."

Jen! Jen was there, too.

Was Jen with Alison? Had Officer Alison figured everything out on her own? Would Sam step out of the pantry to see her best friend in handcuffs?

Sam slowly pulled on her slacks, then pushed open the rickety old pantry door. She stepped out just in time to see her mother race back in from the parking lot. Her mom wasn't in LAPD blues, but she was in the uniform that

Sam had come to recognize as walking-the-beat clothes. Alison wore a straight navy skirt, high-tops and that shapeless beige blazer that was baggy enough to conceal her shoulder holster and her gun.

Sam walked right up to her. "I'm right here," she said nervously. "I've been here the whole time. I was just changing my clothes. I am allowed to do that, aren't I?"

By that time, Jen had joined them. Ms. Sanford and the spirit monsters had gone back to the cafeteria.

"You found out about Jen's car," Sam blurted. She hadn't meant to just blab like that, but there was no more holding back.

"Of course I found out," Alison said. "I've been on the phone all day, questioning students and teachers. Finally, Camille called and told me."

Jen just stared at Sam. Jen was wearing a long jumper and lacy leotard. No handcuffs. Jen looked concerned, but not like someone who was about to be carted off to juvenile court.

Sam stared at Jen. "Camille told you about Jen's car?"

"I already had a lead," Alison answered. "But Camille was able to confirm it. Jen and I talked, and then we headed straight here. Why didn't you tell me, Sam?"

Sam stared at Jen again. She couldn't believe that Jen looked so calm. It was eerie.

Sam was unable to put it together. But before she could ask more questions, Ms.

Sanford stuck her head in. "We're starting the banquet," she said. "Sam, can you still help out here? Do you want me to replace you?"

Sam glanced at her mother, then at Jen.

"I'll help, too," Jen offered. She grabbed an apron.

Sam couldn't put anything together. As if she were sleepwalking, she stuck her hand in her pocket and pulled out the red envelope. She handed it to her mom. "I found this at Kristine Moore's house last night. I don't know who wrote it, or what it means."

Alison took the note. She held onto Sam's hand, forcing Sam to look at her. "Sam," she said in a very serious voice. "I'll tell you everything later. There are still a lot of questions. For now, do your job. Let's get this Award Banquet going. I'll be here the whole time. Jen, you're going to stay, too?"

Jen nodded.

"What's going on?" Sam asked.

Sam saw her mother open her jacket and check her weapon. "Just act normal. Do what you're supposed to do," Alison said. "I'll tell you everything as soon as I can. Let's get this show on the road."

Camille was seated at the head table, between Dylan, Rafe and a huge centerpiece of tissue-paper flowers. Camille was out of the contest, but they'd wanted her to appear with the finalists anyway. Supposedly it was an honor, but all

Camille could think of was some form of exotic torture.

"These five finalists represent excellence in every way," Ms. Sanford was telling the crowd of parents, teachers and friends. Her voice echoed across the cafeteria, wafting through the crepe-paper decorations, the banners and flags. The whole place smelled of onion soup and perfume.

Flash.

"These finalists have been judged on their academic records . . . "

Flash.

"They have been judged on their athletic performance, the contribution each has made to their . . . "

Flash.

The flashes felt like torture to Camille. Or mind control. Three photographers were crouching on the floor right next to Camille, shooting off their strobes like firecrackers.

Flash.

Each time a strobe went off, Camille felt like a zap of electricity had been jolted inside her brain.

"You okay?" Dylan whispered.

Camille had begun to sweat. Her heart was pounding again, and that shallow breathing had begun. She patted her face with her napkin and nodded. But then she glanced at Rafe and realized that she wasn't the only one who was having a hard time.

Rafe was ashen. His blond hair fell over his eyes, and his lips were completely colorless. His knee was jiggling so hard that Camille wondered if he'd knock over the table.

"Nerves," she said. Then she laughed. "Dumb, huh. Why should I be nervous?"

Dylan smiled at her. He didn't look nervous. In fact, he'd eaten most of his dinner. Her chicken and fettucini Alfredo still sat, congealed and looking gray. Barry Barsumian had been the only finalist to ask for seconds. Kristine and Suria had only eaten the low-fat items. Like Camille, Rafe hadn't touched his food.

"Are you okay?" Camille whispered to Rafe.

He didn't even seem to hear her. He was wearing a suit that looked uncomfortable, plus a tie that he kept pulling at, as if he couldn't breathe. Camille could smell sweat, then noticed two wet circles under Rafe's arms.

Flash.

"Rafe, don't worry," Camille whispered, trying to distract herself from the strobe.

He barely seemed to hear her. He didn't seem to be listening to Ms. Sanford either. The person he was staring at was Samantha's mother, who was strolling around the perimeter of the cafeteria, her arms folded across her chest.

Camille turned and stared. What was Alison doing there, Camille wondered. At one point, Sam's mother disappeared into the kitchen, then returned, stowing a police radio in her pocket. Alison stopped in the doorway. She reached in her pocket again and pulled out a red envelope. Then she took the envelope and held it in front of her.

"What's she doing?" Camille whispered, almost to herself.

Ms. Sanford was going on about the Governor's Award, the judges and the rules, but Camille couldn't listen. All Camille could take in was the bizarre sight of Alison holding that red letter, Rafe sweating next to her, and those horrible cameras.

Flash.

Rafe pitched forward over his uneaten food. He stared at Alison. Alison waved the red envelope slightly, and stared back at him.

"Jen's here, too," Camille whispered again, not knowing what else to say. It was as if two totally different scenes were going on at the same time. Ms. Sanford kept talking about the award, while this bizarre silent drama was taking place between Alison and Rafe.

Camille was also surprised to see Jen waiting tables with Sam. Now Jen was clearing, and Sam had disappeared into the kitchen. Camille remembered that Rafe and Jen had been a couple, but also knew that the romance had gone kaput.

Flash.

Make them stop, she wanted to say to Rafe. Instead she whispered, "Good luck."

Rafe let out a tiny grunt.

Camille knew that he wouldn't win. He'd been a strong contender at the top, but he'd lost points consistently since the beginning of the contest. Dylan had beat him at every track meet. Rafe's speech had been unimpressive. Rafe's grades and other accomplishments weren't good enough to make up for those setbacks. Surely Rafe knew that, too. Anybody with any sense knew it was down to Barry, Dylan and Suria.

Flash.

STOP! Camille wanted to demand. She flicked her foot, almost kicking the photographer from the school newspaper and forcing him to crawl back. Then she took a deep breath. She didn't dare indulge in another outburst, lest she get a permanent reputation as a nutcase.

Flash.

"This has been a close contest. We had a sixth finalist who . . . "

Camille knew that Ms. Sanford was referring to her, trying to make up for the fact that she'd dropped out. But with Ms. Sanford's attention came those cameras, all pointed at Camille.

Flash, flash, flash.

Those lights again. Headlights. STOP. Eyes won't focus. Legs won't move. My head, my head, my head . . . Don't you see me? Why won't my legs go? Why don't you stop?

Camille grabbed Rafe's sleeve. He turned to look at her just as another flash went off. That's when the memory came up like something rising from deep, deep water. It felt as if a piece of jagged metal were inside Camille, forcing its way out. Her head hurt and her eyes began to water. Her heart was beating so hard that she felt like she might faint.

Ms. Sanford's microphone rang with feedback.

Camille clapped her hands over her ears.

"And the winner is . . . West L.A. High's newest Governor's Award Recipient . . . "

Flash.

It hurt. The memory hurt Camille's brain. She didn't want to see it. She didn't want to believe it. She didn't want to know. . . .

"The winner is, Mr. Dylan Kussman!"

"Rafe Danielson!" Camille mouthed, feeling like she was going to pass out.

Dylan stood up and waved to his parents, but Rafe just stared at Camille. Then Rafe pushed back his chair, almost plowing into Dylan's legs.

Dylan had won the award, Camille realized. Of course, Dylan had won. But Rafe . . . Rafe Danielson . . .

Flash. Flash.

"Rafe, it was you!" Camille gasped in a barely audible voice. "You drove Jen's car. You hit me and drove away. It was you."

Rafe scrambled backwards. His surfer hair flew, and his tan went pale. Just as Dylan stepped up to the microphone, Rafe put his head back and wailed. It was the moan of some kind of animal. Then he pushed over the table. Dishes crashed. Food covered Suria's skimpy black dress. Ms. Sanford leapt back.

Flash, flash, flash.

"RAFE!" Camille stood up and screamed.

But it was too late. Rafe had already run into the cafeteria kitchen. Alison was running after him, radio in her hand. Jen ran in, too. And no one paid any attention as Dylan stood bewildered, having just won the state's most prestigious student award.

Sam had been changing her clothes again. In that wooden pantry, she'd stood in the dark, just wanting the night to be over and her punishment to be complete. She'd just pulled on her overalls when she heard someone racing back through the kitchen.

"RAFE, STOP!" Sam heard her mother yell.

Then it was a jumble of pots clanging, dishes breaking. A girl screamed and the kitchen door slammed hard.

Sam barely saw him open and close the pantry door. There was just a slice of light, and then she wasn't alone in the small wooden room. Sam had one blink to see Rafe's face, but he didn't look like the Rafe she'd seen around school.

"Rafe, please," she pleaded as she tried to get past him and slip out. He was breathing so hard and the smell of sweat was overwhelming.

Rafe blocked the door. When Sam tried to push by, he picked up a huge can and threw it, right into Sam's thigh.

"*AHHHH*!" Sam screamed.

"SAM!" Alison yelled.

More people were running in the kitchen. More pots were falling. Someone was slamming on the pantry door, while Rafe leaned against it from the inside, breathing so loudly that he didn't even sound human.

"RAFE, OPEN UP. LET SAM OUT," Alison ordered. "I have my gun out, Rafe. I can't let you hurt anyone. If I have to shoot you, I will."

Rafe screamed again, as if he wanted to break the eardrums of the entire world. Then he flailed his strong arms and legs, bashing into what was left on the pantry shelves. Sam stumbled to her knees, covering her face as jars crashed down. Glass shattered. Something heavy slammed into Sam's shoulder and then something wet covered one side of her face.

Sam heard her mother's voice again.

"Camille, get back!" Alison ordered.

And then the pantry door swung open. A startled Camille was standing on the other side. Camille was holding the sink nozzle, pointing the water at Rafe. She managed to spray him hard in the face, even as Alison tried to pull her back.

"NO!" Camille screamed. "I have to do this! Sam come out!"

Rafe scooped up shards of broken glass and threw them at Camille. Camille covered her face and leapt back.

Everyone stepped back now as Rafe was scooping up glass and spilled food, dyed with his own blood that was now pouring out of one wrist. Rafe suddenly stopped when he saw the blood streaming. He turned even paler.

Jen grabbed a towel just as Rafe picked up a knifelike shard of glass and started to slam it down into his bleeding wrist.

"*UGHHHHHHH*," he wailed.

Alison tackled him. He went down hard, so hard that Sam feared he'd cracked his head open on the concrete floor. She saw more blood and prayed that her mom hadn't been cut, too.

Alison and Rafe scrambled. Jen was crying. Sam was shaking. She was suddenly freezing cold and her thigh throbbed. Camille stood very still, staring and ready to take action again.

Then there was a groan and another thump, then a click as Rafe suddenly flopped over on his stomach and two gleaming circles of handcuff were snapped around his blood-covered wrists.

"Just lie still," Alison ordered. She had her radio out and was confirming her call for police backup, plus asking for an ambulance.

Rafe was no longer fighting. He just moaned and rambled, "I want . . . I want to get out of here. I want to die."

Alison sat on top of him, like a big sister in a wrestling match. She took the towel from Jen and tied it tightly around his cut wrist. Finally she touched his bloody face and said, "You're safe now, Rafe. You won't hurt anybody else. You won't hurt yourself. You'll get help, Rafe. Don't worry. I promise. You'll get help."

16

At least Alison had kept him out of juvenile detention. He'd have an arrest record only until he was eighteen. He'd perform community service. If he and his parents continued therapy, he wouldn't go to a juvenile home.

Instead, Rafe Danielson had been taken to Brightwood Canyon, a private treatment center for disturbed teens. Luckily, his parents had money. Otherwise Rafe might have ended up in the psych ward at L.A. General. At least his parents had given him that, Alison told herself. Because as far as she was concerned, the Danielsons hadn't given much else to their desperately troubled son.

Alison sat in Rafe's room at Brightwood. It looked like a college dorm, except for the blank walls and the observation window in the door. The center was set back in the woods of Topanga Canyon, so that it had a summer camp feel, too.

Rafe, however, looked anything but free and easy. He sat at a desk chair, across from Alison. His wrist was bandaged and there were other cuts on his handsome face. Wearing a tee shirt and sweat pants, he stared out through the window bars.

Under the surfer image and all the accomplishments was a history of loneliness and rage. Rafe had admitted that he'd set things on fire at home. Small things, that he could keep under control. Bundles of newspaper. Bathroom towels. In a fit of rage, he'd destroyed his mother's garage art studio, then blamed it on a vandal. He had terrible nightmares and had tried to hurt himself several times.

There was also a history of what Alison considered abuse. In Rafe's case, the abuse wasn't physical. Rafe's parents never hit him, or burned him, or locked him in a dark room. But they didn't do much else either. They withheld. That was their way of showing their disapproval. When Rafe misbehaved, his parents stopped speaking to him. For weeks. They wanted excellence, and only rewarded Rafe when he excelled. They hadn't shown up at the Awards Banquet, because Rafe had admitted that he didn't think he was going to win. They'd only come down to the center on orders from the psychiatrist.

"So at the dance, three weeks ago, you danced with Jennifer Dubrosky," Alison prompted. He'd already confessed in front of two detectives and a court-appointed lawyer. She'd just dropped in to check on him, but he'd wanted to tell his story, again and again. He wanted someone to listen.

"Yeah, yeah, the dance," Rafe rambled. His face looked so young, and his hair still gleamed. He rocked slightly and rubbed his arms, as if he were cold. "I liked Jen. I'd just found out that I'd made the finals for the Governor's Award, but then I'd lost the meet. I was really upset about that. But Jen didn't seem to care. I guess . . . "

"Jen has been through some hard times, too," Alison confirmed.

Rafe nodded. "Jen was coming on pretty strong, and I was feeling so strung out. I didn't want to be alone, and Jen said we could leave the dance together. But first, she wanted to check in with her friends. So she gave me her car keys. I told her I'd get her car, come back and pick her up."

"And then what happened?"

"This girl, Caroline, she'd brought a bottle of whisky. Jen didn't see me drinking, and I drank kind of as much as I could, just chugged it really fast. I just felt like I was going nuts, and the booze kind of calmed me down."

"And then you went and got Jen's car?"

"I guess I was drunk. I didn't think I was drunk, but I must have been driving fast. I was only driving the car from the street into the school parking lot. Maybe I wasn't paying attention either, and it was really dark. And then out of nowhere, this girl was in the street . . . "

"You mean Camille."

"I didn't know it was Camille. I didn't see

her until she was right there, and it was too late to stop. I tried to stop. I never would want to hit anyone. And then it happened. It happened so fast, and I didn't know what to do. It was like my whole life just stopped. I was just barely holding it together before that. I wanted to die right there. I should have gotten out and helped her, but I was so scared . . . "

"So what did you do?"

Rafe took a trembly breath. "I drove about a block away, and then I turned the car around, and I drove it right back to where it had been parked before. I threw the keys in the front seat, then I ran home."

"So Jen just thought you'd stood her up."

"I guess. I wouldn't talk to her after that. I guess she just thought I'd dumped her, but I couldn't face her. I didn't know if I could face anyone. I didn't tell anyone, which made me feel like I was going to explode."

"And then?"

"I felt like I was going totally nuts," Rafe told her. "I kept working on my stuff for the Governor's Award, and my parents kept talking about how I was going to win."

"You stole the books from Kristine?"

Rafe nodded. "I was so angry and scared, and I heard Kristine bragging about how she was going to win because she'd found these great books. And I knew if I didn't win, my parents would hate me, so I slammed off Kristine's lock with a screwdriver from shop class, and then I took her books and threw them away."

"What about the spirit sign?" Alison asked.

"That was because of my meet. I kept losing my track meets, and I just wanted to tell someone about the accident. I wanted somebody to find out. So I went back to the stadium and spray painted that sign in broad daylight. I sat there and waited. I was sure somebody would figure it out. But nobody saw me. Nobody cared!"

Alison touched his hand. He had started to cry. "And then you messed up your Governor's Award speech, right?"

"My parents were there. Every time I looked at them I thought about the car accident. I knew somebody would figure out that it was me, and I knew I could never pull off this award. And my father had actually helped me with my speech. For once, he'd really gotten into it. And then I got up there and I kind of blanked, and I skipped a big part. Nobody else knew I messed it up. But my dad knew. And when I did that, I saw my dad and my mom just get up and walk out. They made a point of it, letting me know that I'd let them down."

Alison felt sick. "They walked out? They walked out in the middle of your speech?"

His bandaged hand was clenched in a fist. "To show me how badly I'd screwed up, I guess. That's their big thing, to let me know when I'm a big screw-up." He almost smiled. "I wonder what they think now."

"Rafe, did you smash the trophy case?"

He held up his hand. "I just wrapped my jacket around my hand and slammed the glass.

Then I took out my trophy and . . . I wanted to kill myself. If I'd had the guts, I would have done it, because I knew I was going nuts, man. I knew I couldn't stand it much longer. And I didn't care anymore. I was starting to feel so alone and so angry, and nobody was paying attention. I tried leaving a note at that party. I didn't know what else to do. I just wanted somebody to listen to me . . . but nobody noticed . . . nobody would catch me, or talk to me or know what I'd done. . . ."

That same afternoon, Sam sat alone on the lawn in front of her apartment building. She noticed everything. Each car that passed by on Spaulding Avenue seemed to tell its own little story—Beamer with skis and a car phone, wannabe starlet in a Honda Civic, Volvo full of rowdy kids.

The kids waved at Sam and made faces. Sam waved back, then just sat, taking it all in. The air was amazingly clear for L.A. Sam could smell the grass, the car exhaust and the curry someone was simmering across the street. She enjoyed the way the sun beat down on her bare shoulders. For the first time in weeks, she felt sane.

Maybe it was just the suntan weather, and the lack of smog. Maybe it was finally knowing who had caused so much trouble at school. Sam felt confident that Jen was going to be okay. Camille would recover, too. Maybe some day their entire school would feel right again.

Sam closed her eyes and let her head fall back. The sun made her face feel tight, but it also eased the pain in her leg and her side. She'd almost fallen asleep when she heard the sound. She didn't have to open her eyes to identify it. The *putt-putt* sound was a cross between a lion purr and the sound of a remote-controlled plane.

It was Kenny pulling up on the Motogoozi, his red Italian motor scooter. There probably wasn't another scooter like it in all of L.A.

Sam lifted her head and just barely squinted as he climbed off it, then leaned the scooter against a telephone pole. Kenny spotted her immediately, but she pretended not to notice him. Through eyelids like slits, she saw his wild hair backlit by the bright sun, and his tee shirt that said, "Reality Check." He strode up the walkway, carting a soft guitar case and loping in that goofy, long-legged way of his.

As he came closer, Sam lowered her face. She picked grass and built a tiny cut-grass mountain. By the time he was within a few feet of her, he knew that something was up. She wasn't acting like the good old normal Sam. She didn't even say hello.

Kenny stopped. He circled around her like he was beginning some kind of war dance. Finally he put down his guitar and sat next to her. He imitated her posture. Crossed legs. Straight back. Eyes down. Then he pinched some of her pulled grass and sprinkled it over the top of her head.

Sam flinched and brushed the grass off. She started for the apartment lobby door.

"That's mature," Kenny said, stopping her in her tracks.

"Who ever said I was mature," Sam tossed back, not looking at him. She could see his reflection in the glass window that was inset in the lobby door. His hair looked electric and his bony shoulder poked through the back of his shirt.

"Well, join the immaturity club," he said. He picked more grass and threw it up in the air like confetti. "After this weekend, I think I win the prize as club president."

Sam slowly turned around and leaned back against the apartment door. "And why is that?"

He didn't answer right away. "This was one pretty weird weekend. I heard about Danielson. Whoa."

"My mom's with him right now," Sam said coolly. "She'll be home soon."

Kenny stared out at the street. "What about you? Did you do anything crazy this weekend?"

"*Moi?* Not me. At least not any crazier than I've been for the last few weeks. How about you?"

"*Moi*, too?"

"Kenny."

He turned around and tried to give her a stupid smile.

She glared.

"I'll tell you about it sometime," he mumbled.

"You don't have to," she confirmed. "I saw everything. At least I hope I saw everything."

Kenny jumped up. He was covered with grass. "You saw!"

"I saw. You conquered."

"Oh no," Kenny moaned. He rushed up to her. "It was a mistake, Sam. I was temporarily insane. I was duped. I'm an idiot. Were you there? Did someone tell you? I didn't think anybody saw. How did you know?"

She decided not to tell him. She just smirked. "I saw. And I understand."

"You do?" he gawked. "Could you explain it to me?"

Suddenly Sam was tired of this game. She was sick of insane secrets and not knowing what was going on. "No, that's not true, Kenny. I don't understand. How could you do it? What's going on? So are you and Kristine some big item now? What do you see in her? How could you do that to me?"

"To you?" he gasped. "TO YOU! I never know where I stand with you. You're always off with Dylan. I feel like I'm just standing around, being back up, being your second choice when he doesn't show up."

"At least Dylan isn't a creep!" Sam argued.

Kenny stuck his face in hers. "Yeah, yeah. Mr. Hero Governor's Award of California."

"Miss Social Queen Creep of West L.A. High."

"Hey, hey." Kenny threw up his hands. "Kristine threw herself at me."

"Kenny."

"I'm irresistible."

"You're a jerk."

"That, too."

He tousled her hair.

She punched him. Then she pulled back. "Enough violence." She touched the huge purple bruise on her thigh. "Enough craziness. Enough secrets. I'm hungry. I don't want to do this anymore." She unlocked the lobby door. "Let's talk later, okay, Kenny?"

"Okay," he sighed.

Sam went in and climbed the stairs, leaving him alone in the lobby. "I just want to keep feeling sane."

Alison came home before dinnertime.

Sam was curled up on the couch, finishing her homework. "How was it?" she asked.

Alison dumped her purse in the foyer, then sat down next to Sam. She took off her jacket. She wasn't wearing her gun. "Depressing."

"Will Rafe make it? Does he have a chance?"

"I hope so. I don't know though. I'm hungry."

Sam smiled. She wasn't just hungry, she realized. She was empty. She needed her friends. She needed her mom. She needed a sane life that could fill her up again. "El Tapatio?" she suggested in a timid voice.

Alison thought for a minute.

"I think it's a good idea," Sam said.

"You owe me a dinner, this time," Alison said and laughed.

"Let's just eat."

"And talk."

"And eat."

"And listen," Alison said.

"And eat."

Alison suddenly hugged Sam so hard that Sam almost couldn't breathe. Then Alison pulled back and smiled. "Let's just spend some time together."

"Okay."

"I love you, Sam," Alison promised. Her eyes filled with tears. "I want to be here for you. I know it hasn't been easy since I've taken this job."

Sam felt the tug of tears, too. It hadn't been easy. In fact, she sometimes felt like the LAPD had committed the crime of stealing her mom. Sam stood up and pulled her mom up, too. "Come on. I don't want to sit here and cry, Mom. I'm starving. I want to eat. . . "

"And talk."

"And talk."

"And eat. . . "

They both laughed and headed for the door.